I0647259

The Married LIFE

Living In Fullness Everyday

By

Anthony Lamar Smith

ISBN: 978-1-7341488-2-4

Front cover image by Tyler Nicols.
Book design by Tyler Nichols.
www.tylertreats.com

Printed by, Inc., in the United States of America.

First printing edition 2020.

LIFE Impact Plus

16787 Beach Blvd

Huntington Beach, CA 92647

www.antlamarsmith.com

We hope you enjoy this book from LIFE Publishing. Our goal is to provide high-quality, thought-provoking books and products that connect truth to your real needs and challenges. For more information on other books and products written and produced by LIFE Publishing, go to www. Or write to:

LIFE Impact Plus

16787 Beach Blvd

Huntington Beach, CA 92647

A word from the author

I cannot fully articulate the joy it gives me to share my heart with you, and I am honored that you have shared your time with me by reading this book. I am grateful and my soul rejoices. It is my prayer that you will evolve into the person that God created you to be and that you will manifest the type of marriage and relationship that the Creator intends for you.

Other books by **Anthony Lamar Smith**

Twitter: **@AntLamarSmith**
Facebook: **AntLamarSmith**
Instagram: **AnthonyLamarSmith**

Purpose of book: To help couples and those who desire to be married

1) **ReVive** your marriage

2) **ReCreate** the vision for your marriage

3) **ReDistribute** your daily efforts towards creating and experiencing the marriage of your dreams

You deserve to live...

ACKNOWLEDGEMENT

To the Love of My Life, you are the inspiration behind this book. Your love, loyalty, wit and intelligence, and unwavering natural beauty both physically and spiritually are why I was compelled to create this masterpiece. Our love story began long before we met in this lifetime. Our adventure expands throughout multiple life experiences and transcends eternity. When you and I "reconnected" in 2011, my heart knew immediately that it had found its home. Living inside of our Utopia feels safe and loving. Our intimacy is what inspires romance novels and box-office romantic comedies. Until our hearts reunited I was completely unaware of what 'true love' is or meant. And it was at that moment that I realized the truth and what it means to find my soul mate. You make my heart smile. And you bring so much joy to my entire Being. Sharing my life with you is an honor, a privilege, and eternal bliss. And I am grateful to unveil our story with the rest of the world, so that they may also be inspired and encouraged, while applying the principles that ignited our passion and have kept the flames burning since the beginning of infinity.

Thank You Shira Nicole Smith for being my wife. I love you baby!

Contents

Anthony Lamar Smith
Shira Nicole Smith

"We Are One"

As I gaze into the eyes of the mirror that looks back at me
I see my reflection through the eyes that's looking through me.
He sees the beauty of who I am with my own vision
He touches me with every caress of my hands upon my figure.

He tastes me with each glide of my tongue across my lips
and can smell me as my natural fragrance emits into the air.
He hears me speak as the melody of my voice
dances across my eardrums.

As I shower I can feel the drops of a thousand of his touches
while the sensation of his hands drips down my anatomy.
When I am dressed I am clothed in his everlasting embrace.
And he loves me even more with the more that I love myself.

As I spray the fragrance from this crystal perfume bottle
I am entranced by thoughts of each time our bodies are drawn
together; now I wear the scent of his passion upon me.

As I think he becomes more educated
His salvation is rooted in my prayers, calmness and peace rest
upon him during my times of meditation.
He is at peace when I am at peace...
and excited when I am excited!
As I travel about my day I realize that I am not alone...
for He is with me.

Who Am I...I am Shira Nicole Smith
Who Is He...He is Anthony Lamar Smith
Who Are We...We Are ONE!

The Married LIFE | *Anthony Lamar Smith*

CHAPTER 1

I HATE YOU: Sean and Aliyah

My father told me that *"Happily, Ever After"* is an illusion. He said that no marriage is happy, and that couples who wed only marry so that they don't find themselves living and dying alone. He often stated to my siblings and I that women marry men with jobs who can take care of her, and men marry women to take care of his kids and do all the shit that a man doesn't want to do when he comes home from work.

"Son, marriage is like a national holiday; the good times only come around once in a while. Every now and then, like Christmas or your birthday, those particular days may feel exciting, but all of the other days are just normal, nothing to boast about. Seriously, most days are kind of boring or routine to be honest, Sean."

As he elaborated the advice he was giving me seemed foolish, yet at that time for some reason it felt like his logic made sense. Honestly, if he weren't my dad I wouldn't have even given his marital philosophy any of my attention.

Placing his hand on my shoulder while we sat on the front porch of my childhood home smoking a cigar, drinking whiskey, and enjoying the warm summer evening, his voice raspy from old age he said,

"just like your mom and I, as long as you understand this and never have any high expectations, your marriage will last until the day you die."

I sat next to him motionless, staring off into the dark spaces of my mind while contemplating if his opinions are partly the reason why my marriage failed.

My father was a very practical man, dull; nothing exciting about him. Which is why to me, for almost five decades my mother seemed disinterested with their relationship. He was a realist, and never deviated from his routines. Very predictable. His primary goal while raising his children was for us to experience life without any high expectations so that we would never feel disappointed if things didn't work out.

I, however, am more of an optimist and had an appetite for variety and excitement. I made a vow when I was a young boy witnessing their interactions that my marriage would be nothing like my parents. Forty-seven years later, my folks are still living "unhappily, ever after". Once, looking into my mother's eyes, it appeared that she'd been miserable for so long that she probably wouldn't recognize *happiness* if it were staring her in the face. Perhaps it's not misery; maybe it's loneliness. Or could it be both? Once, shortly after their 35th anniversary, after a heated argument with my dad, my mother told me that she stayed with him because she felt she had no choice.

"Back in my day, when I married your father, women never really believed in the fairy-tale marriages that were shown on television. The storylines looked good on TV, my girlfriends and I would sometimes fantasize what it would be like to have that type of marriage, but we knew that it wasn't a reality for us. Protect your heart Sean, and remember your vows, for better or worse, richer or poorer, and sickness or in health", my mother said to me. "Your marriage will never become a nightmare if you never believe in the dream."

Today her advice feels bizarre realizing that the *American Dream* that I once shared with Aliyah, twelve years later, has been rewritten into an *American Horror*

Story. But unlike the 1984 popular thriller *"Nightmare on Elm Street"*, our horror story didn't premier last Friday. The villain that has slashed away our joy and terrorized our relationship over the past eight years made living in this marriage feel like a frightening ordeal, for both of us.

When I married my wife, I sure as hell didn't marry her for *"worse, poorer, or sickness"*. Let's be honest, no one does. At the altar I stood with a perfectly healthy woman, rich with ideas and dreams of our future, who made me feel that my latter days would be made better because of her.

On our wedding day I set out to prove to my parents that their advice was wrong, but over these past few years daily life in my marriage seemed to prove that what they advised was right.

But there has to be a *system* to a good marriage. I crave adventure and excitement, but like my father I am also a practical guy. Just give me the rules to a happy marriage and I'll adhere to them. I just need a step-by-step plan that I can follow consistently. However, it appears that all of the tips, suggestions, ideas and opinions that I have received or witnessed throughout my life of this so-called *system to marital bliss* has proven that the traditional methods to a successful marriage is obviously broken.

Why is *"happily, ever after"* synonymous with marriage when statistics seem to highlight that the majority of married couples who don't divorce are not happy in their marriage at all?

Who was the idiot that started this propaganda? And is it possible to enjoy a drama free marriage *"until death do you part"*. There is no benefit to wearing a frown upon my face throughout my marriage and a smile on my face while lying in a coffin. My wife and I want to be happy with each other right now.

I have taken the painful lessons from my failed marriage and by learning from other married couples, specifically people in successful marriages who are living happily, discovered a few key principles that if applied regularly will lead to living your best marriage possible.

Here is how it all began....

Summer 2008

For a while everyone but Aliyah and I said that our relationship was puppy love. No one thought that we would actually marry, and when we did they certainly didn't believe that it would last forever. Several years into our marriage I admit I was the first to fall out of love. And I didn't even know it. We married young, barely 19, old enough to join the military but still not quite grown enough to buy alcohol. Looking back, I now realize how naive we were. It takes a lot of arrogance to think that you can be happily married to the *same* person for fifty or more years. Think about this for a moment, how egotistical is that. But I'm a proud and vain man, I promised myself that no matter how unhappy Aliyah and I may become, like our parents we are not going to dissolve this marriage. My mindset was that even if the love wanes, the competition must continue so that instead of our friends and family, we will get *the last laugh*. But over time the jealousy and insecurity in our relationship became antagonizing. Every little thing seemed to spark a war, but there was no alcohol in our cupboards that could drown out the tension that seemed to infiltrate our home. This is weird because when we started dating during the spring of 1995, and spoke our vows July 13, 1996 I thought that I was madly in love with her. Turns out that I wasn't, and like many other young men I had confused lust for love.

And I'll admit, they were exciting times, the late 90s and early 2000s. We were a blossoming family of four living the American dream in the northern suburbs of Chicago. Aliyah and I had been married for six years, created the ideal family with our 4-year-old son Sean Jr. and 6 months old daughter Maraya, and last month we closed escrow on our dream home, a 2-story Craftsman-style house complete with 5 bedrooms 4 bathrooms, 3300 square feet of living space on a half-acre of land all before my 25th birthday. Achieving this lifestyle was made possible four years earlier when I started my career in the real estate industry at twenty-one and created a real estate brokerage and partnership by the time I was twenty-three.

Our current lifestyle is a vast contrast from being raised in a three-bedroom one-bathroom 1690 sq. feet bungalow on the south side of Chicago where I lived with my parents, my sister Shanice, two brothers Michael and Dylan, and my mom's youngest brother. Terrell moved in with us right after my grandmother became ill from a stroke and was no longer able to care for him. He was born seven months before me and although we were raised as siblings, my uncle Terrell is also my best friend.

My parents shared a bedroom; and because she's the only female child my sister had a bedroom to herself. Because of our crowded home I require lots of living space, I have very little patience and oftentimes need to distance myself from everyone, and I absolutely despise conflict. I purposely bought a house with more bedrooms than needed for our little family of four because I spent my entire childhood crammed into the last available bedroom with three other male occupants. The space was confined, and as you can imagine the confrontations were often.

Aliyah also grew up in a house with both parents, but her childhood was plagued with drama and turmoil. Her mother was a Corrections Officer at the Cook County Jail and her father worked construction as a General Contractor. Neither had any college education, but were very hard workers. Employed in a violent environment and interacting with criminal offenders for 10-12 hours each day, Aliyah's mom had a way with words. Her lexicon was complete with every foul expression both written and imagined, and she never held back when given the opportunity to articulate this vernacular to anyone and everyone. She was notorious for dropping the F-bomb and calling her kids by names that would never be legally allowed on a birth certificate. As a toddler and adolescent Aliyah thought that *Lil' Bitch* was her nickname.

Unlike my parents who appeared complacent and bored with each other, Aliyah's mom and dad seemed entertained by the constant fights and arguments; it's almost as if they were aroused by drama, as if conflict was a type of aphrodisiac. I've known her parents for almost two decades and never have I been in their presence while being captivated by an aura of peace and tranquility. Just saying hello was met with a look that implied *'why the fuck is you so damn happy'*. Being insulted and yelled at were dubbed as "acts of affections". Silence meant disinterest, and if they weren't talking shit about you it meant that they didn't like you. Confusing? Absolutely. Conditioned by constant dysfunction, anything contrary seemed abnormal.

When Aliyah's mom knew that her disciplinary tactics had gone too far she would lavish her kids with money and expensive gifts in an attempt to beseech their forgiveness. Aliyah and my brother-in-law always wore the latest sneakers and trendy fashions, but underneath her fancy garb were scares from physical and emotional abuse. And even while wearing her new shoes, around her mom it was like walking on eggshells, anything could set her off causing a jail-like riot outrage that would last for hours. To escape, she would lock herself in her bedroom curled up under her favorite blanket and nose deep in a novel.

Her upbringing led to major issues in our marriage. I truly believe that she suffers from undiagnosed PTSD brought about by years of prolonged emotional and physical traumatic experiences. At times outward appearances were deceiving, but her childhood was not easy. And growing up on the west side of Chicago added to here post-traumatic stress disorder.

Chicago, IL, a city known for its meticulous landscape and architectural marvels, and is one of the most popular tourist destinations in the United States. But a short distance from the magic of the beautiful lakefront skyline, fabulous restaurants, and world-class shopping exist a microcosm grappled with violence that in some years claim more than 500 murders, according to the

Chicago Sun-Times. Living in one of the most besieged communities in Chicago, you can imagine how difficult it was for Aliyah and her family when her brother was killed by gun violence while sitting in his car with his girlfriend during spring break 1994. Losing her brother was devastating. She never received counseling to handle the pain, and considers the loss of *anything* as comparable to the death of her brother. During her senior year of high school, she lost her job as a waitress at Applebee's restaurant, and for almost three months she cried, grieved, and mourned that event.

Aliyah was very careful to never react to our children the way her mom responded to she and her brother, but she never failed short of talking to or belittling me as if I was also her mother's child. At such a young age, she and I weren't even mature enough for the demands of *adulthood*, that alone the requirements of a marriage in its infancy. Marriage during the newlywed phase is similar to the first twenty-four months of raising a newborn child. It is extremely taxing and requires a lot of love, attention, and patience. And the biggest challenge during the new stage of marriage is that each person tends to bring into the relationship what they witness and endured during their parent's marriage.

Dysfunction breeds more dysfunction. Like attracts like. Broken people are drawn to broken people. Like magnates, people are attracted to folks that are just like themselves, or to people whom they want to be just like. She and I growing up in socially impaired homes was the "perfect storm" for a disastrous marriage. She was drawn to my "calm demeanor" that I actually hid very well until something forced me to react irrationally. And I was attracted to all of her spectacles that seemed to add a bit of adventure and excitement to my life. My mother once told me that *"people become what they hate the most"*. In other words, you will manifest in your life what you emotionally give the most attention. The very things I hated about Aliyah's mom, I became. Over time our marriage resembled what we loathed about our parents, and as you probably assume, that shit became boring real fast and we started resenting each other and abhorred all of the melodrama that ravaged our relationship.

The Moment We Knew Our Marriage Was Over

Pulling into the driveway one mid-August evening in 2008, I saw my wife standing on the porch with her arms crossed and looking agitated. The look upon her face simulated the blazing heat from the torturous 103-degree temperature that afternoon. The steam resonating from the top of her head reminds me of the humidity that never seems to dissipate throughout these summer time evenings in Chicago.

What a contrast, her standing in front of our meticulously landscaped home complete with some of my favorite flowers. The white and yellow daisies and daylilies, purple geraniums, and the red cardinal flowers are reminiscent of how I used to see her; beautiful, slim, vibrant, with a nectar-like personality that draws everyone into her presence. But I can tell from the energy spewing out of her that this was going to be another evening where the poisonous weeds deeply rooted in my garden would choke the life out of my delicate flowers.

We argued and fought mostly about my loyalty to her and our marriage. She doesn't feel that I love her anymore, that I am disinterested with the daily routines, and can sense that I want to dissolve our relationship. But the truth is that I am terrified because when I look at myself in the mirror I can see in my eyes the same loneliness that I saw in my mother's. And I am unaware of any optical wear that can improve the vision that I have of this marriage.

This time she's upset because I didn't answer her repeated calls and countless text messages throughout the day. Indeed, being an at-home mom and tending to the needs of our children and household can be challenging, but I am not in the mood to listen to this shit or her bitching about it for what feels like the one-millionth time.

>	*"I can't stand you Sean", she yelled. "I fucking hate you!"*

I could sense the atmospheric energy shift, but even more in my soul because I was frustrated by how arduous it felt to be in this marriage. And at that moment every ill emotion that I had buried inside of me began to rise to the surface because our matrimony feels like the longest war in American history. Even worse is that our children are also casualties of this vicious and unrelenting battle.

But it wasn't always like this. Where did we go wrong? With all of our history, all of the issues we've overcome, and goals we have achieved, I now spend my evenings in my "man cave" that's complete with a home theater and wet bar. And she spends the evenings attending to our children or curled up on a chaise in the solarium with a glass of Cabernet Sauvignon in one hand and a romance novel in the other.

Seeing her reading these damn fictional tales irritates the fuck out of me, but I remember the days when I treasured those moments of seeing her enwrapped by the oversized chaise with her favorite chinchilla blanket draped across her body. She once looked so sweet to me. Her beauty was radiant and she looked very innocent, yet I was enticed by her *bad girl* persona. Now when I see her reading all I imagine is that she's comparing what she is *not* getting from me to the fantasy perfect husband drafted between 300 pages of some author's fancy.

We used to have so much fun together. Maybe because we were college kids back then. It seemed like our life together was better when we were financially broken and struggling, or pursuing some ambition. Perhaps, now that we are in our thirties and living an accomplished life, we no longer have anything else to aspire towards. We don't share any more goals. Maybe we're sick and tired of each other. Can it be that we have grown apart? We both feel lonely and trapped in the mundane routines of what has become our life. This isn't fun anymore.

"Sean, you knew that I was supposed to go out with Sharon and Tiana today.

Aliyah, Sharon and Tiana have been best friends since the 3rd grade, and they are practically inseparable. An argument with my wife means a beef with all three of them. My wife tells her friends every goddamn thing about our relationship, every fucking detail. And I'm sure tonight's little get-together would be all about "their" issues with me.

"This is my one night of the week to be without the kids. I don't ask much from you. You're hardly home and barely spend any time with YOUR children; the least that

you could do is give me this ONE night to go out with my friends. You make me sick! Tiana and Sharon were right; I should've never married you. You're selfish, you are so stupid and only think about yourself. I've been stuck in this goddamn house all day with these kids. Mommy, Mommy, Mommy is all I hear from sun up to sun down. I never get a break. I'm going fucking crazy!" she continued yelling.

Aliyah was insistent and kept nagging, pushing, berating and hitting me, as she did often; doing all that she could to get me to battle with her. The more I resisted, even more the negative energy inside of me boiled over until I finally retaliated as if she were one of my brothers.

"I fucking hate you too! But even worse is that I have animosity towards myself for once loving you. You are the woman that I hate...to love."

I paused so that she could feel my intensity. My intention was to hurt her. My stomach churned, and just looking at her was nauseating.

My tonality is low and my vibrations reminiscent of her mom, I said to her *"you're so ugly to me, and I can't believe that I even entertained the idea that you were pretty, that you were attractive, or sexy."*

"I hate being with you, being around you, and having sex with you. And now yelling I said to her *"your very presence irritates the fuck out of me, you Lil' Bitch."*

It seemed that the walls of our house began to rattle and the lights flickered, and a deathly silence fell upon the room. A look of shock and awe was drawn upon her face; she was taken aback by what I said to her. In her heart she could feel that I was indeed disgusted with her and no longer desired to be her *"lawfully wedded husband"*. *"To hold and to cherish"* meant her clamping her hands upon my larynx, squeezing with the force of a pair of vice-grips, and taking delight as the final *breath of life* expels from my body, as she witnesses *death do us part.*

"I abhor you, despise you, and utterly dislike you. I knew when I said I Do; I heard the voice of my heart say...

"But, I Don't".

Streams of tears rolled down her face, and even I began to cry because the intensity of this particular fight was unwarranted. But this time, some of my tears are actually tears of joy. After *twelve years a slave* to this marriage we should have finally figured out how to "live happily, ever after". Some couples pray and meditate each morning, but fights and verbal assaults were our daily ritual. However, this argument was different, because at that time the words spewing out of my mouth was how I truly felt about our marriage.

As the fight continued, I was ferocious and allowed my true feelings to be expressed.

"You are a fucking imbecile, and an irritation to my soul. The very essence of my entire Being is absolutely disgusted with this marriage and from henceforth it is over, bitch.

You hate me, I'm sure for many reasons. But I hate you because I despise myself for lying that I could possibly live happily the rest of my life with you;" I said to her in a callous manner.

The tranquility in my voice felt strange because of the odious energy that was just present in the room. But there is something about the truth that causes evil to dissipate. I had finally released the truth of how I felt about being married to her. Although she was crying wholeheartedly, at that moment I personally felt the happiest I had been since before our nuptials. In front of 38 guests, I stood with her and lied that our marriage would last *"till death do us part"*. But the truth is that our marriage was dead on arrival.

As I stormed out of the house, she pursued while imploring me not to leave. The weeks passed with constant phone calls and messages of her seeking reconciliation, and oh how I also wanted to so badly for the sake of our children. But I just could not convince myself to heed her request. Gallivanting about my day relishing in my newfound personal freedom, like a hummingbird drawn to the nectar of a red cardinal flower, the appeal of living my life as a bachelor was too tantalizing for me to resist. The decision to divorce was finalized in my heart, and my mind made up that I would never get married again.

The constant demands for your time, being accountable for other people, doing for your spouse tasks that you don't want to do. The labor, the effort, the chore...I agree with what countless husbands and wives around the world have confirmed, ***"marriage is hard work"***

...so I thought.

I Love You, but I Don't Like You

Something that I learned during our separation is that there is a vast difference between *loving* the one you're with, and *liking* the one you're with. It is often said that when couples fall out of love the relationship is over. And it is also said that "love is powerful" and (as written in the Weymouth New Testament Bible, 1 Peter 4:8) *"Above all continue to love one another fervently, for love throws a veil over a multitude of faults.*

But in my opinion, this scripture is limited because couples that actually love each other sometimes fall apart or divorce; and many married people that were never truly *intimately in love* with each other stay married until the day they die. How can two people in love end up in divorce? Well there is an easy answer to this question, it's because they dislike each other.

Love won't keep a relationship together when the two of you don't even like one another.

Aliyah and I were once in love and now we no longer *like* each other the way we did when we were dating in college. Our relationship has descended into a *DISLIKE* state. There's 'love' for one another because of the longevity of our relationship, but if we're honest with ourselves we haven't liked each other in a long time. *'I LOVE you, but I don't LIKE you' has* become the reality for our relationship.

She *DISLIKED* being around me because my patience is short and I get irritated quickly. I *DISLIKED* spending time together without the kids to keep me entertained and distracted. We *DISLIKED* talking to each other or even hearing the other person's voice. We have limited our time together in exchange for more time with our friends. WHY...because we *LIKE* our friends. Aliyah likes how her friends make her feel, and how being in their presence refreshes, recharges and refuels her the way I once did.

During a conversation with a female colleague a few weeks ago, our talk and the energy exchanged was a reminder of how being LIKED feels exhilarating, it's invigorating, and makes you feel enlivened. The social media *"LIKE"* button is what has made Facebook so popular. Instagram's popularity fails in comparison; someone pushing the *LOVE* button doesn't have the same emotional impact because the term *LOVE* has become such a cliché.

But to be LIKED means that you *enjoy or are fond of me;* we're compatible; and have similarities; and maybe we're exactly alike. Most of us feel that if I LIKE myself, everyone else would be fond of me too. You LIKE my thoughts and ideas; you appreciate who I am as a person. You adore me the way that I admire you. You LIKE me as a friend; which is why I sent or accepted your social media friend request.

Sometimes being LIKED feels better than being LOVED. I love my brother, but I thought that Aliyah would be that friend who *"sticks closer than a brother."*

Valuable lesson learned, but the marriage is over now. I do not desire to reconcile nor do I have an appetite to ever remarry. Being in this marriage has left an unpleasant aftertaste upon my palate. However, in my future, unrecognizable to me, off in the distance, just over the horizon, what seemed almost naked to the human eye, a new life happily and eagerly awaited my arrival.

CHAPTER 2:

Marriage is Not Hard Work
Oliver and Elizabeth

"Only fools marry, Bro. I'm living my best life possible, 'singlely ever after'. S.I.N.G.L.E.L.Y", he spelled out slowly. *And if you ever think about doing that marriage crap again I'll divorce you myself. I will take you to court and ask for a friendship annulment on the grounds of you being a dumb ass."*

Terrell, my uncle and best friend is known for "keeping it real", as they say in the hood. One evening during our fitness training session at the gym while referring to my marriage he took delight in reminding me that he was the first to tell me not to marry Aliyah.

"Singlely, what the hell is singlely; that's not a word", I said as we both laughed hysterically.

"Sure it is, look it up in the Urban Dictionary. It means, 'Happily single 'til the day you die.' And that's me, Bro. To hell with that marriage foolishness; I'm a playa for life."

Laughing and looking at him while shaking my head in disagreement; *"By the way, the word is singly, fool; not singlely. But you're going to take me to court for being a dumb ass,"* I said while looking at him with a scowl upon my face.

This philosophy that marriage is hard work is such an unfortunate reality for so many spouses. Some of the reasons are because far too often people marry out of protocol, convenience, or necessity. With my marriage and those that I've witnessed during childhood and until now, it seems that very few couples actually marry because they are truly in love with each other; or sincerely desire to evolve into their best selves with one another; or even know the spiritual benefits of marriage.

I learned this lesson the hard way with my previous relationship. It's been three years since Aliyah and I divorced, and the separation has been agonizing. Every so often I still relive the pain of our breakup and miss the happier times of our relationship. I've asked myself was I really miserable, or is it that I am feeling lonely now. Or, perhaps like my mother, it's both?

Divorce is traumatic, an ordeal that I do not wish upon anyone. And it's bewildering as well. Because you're supposed to be happy that the relationship is over, yet your essence and every part of you wants to run back to the confinement of what once felt like wearing a straitjacket and being locked in a room with padded walls and no windows. The adage "there is always a light at the end of a dark tunnel" sounds good. But enduring the hellish adventures along the journey to the other side is not for the weak-hearted. One does not *get* a divorce; you go *through* it; it is suffering and sobering simultaneously. Divorce is harrowing, harsh, and tortuous. Like losing a loved one, you grieve the passing away of what was once a *holy matrimony*. Marriage and divorce are both something that I espoused to never again participate.

During a week in February 2010 while on a business trip in Orlando, I became acquainted with this wonderfully charming couple. They were sitting on a bench holding hands and gazing out upon Lake Willis. The scene was fanciful with the golden glow of the evening sunset shining across the water. There was a light breeze, the palm trees swayed in an almost choreographed dance, families enjoying water activities on the lake, music playing in the background and the chatter and laughter of children added a cozy family-oriented feeling to the moment. In a flash I began to grieve this scene because I was missing my children. The four of us had such a great time when we visited Disneyworld almost five years ago. I was heartbroken, but nonetheless, the evening was picturesque.

Looking around at the many families celebrating quality time together, I was drawn to this lovely couple that appeared to be in their late eighties, and inquired of how long they have been married.

"Sixty-two years' young man", said the elderly man named Oliver.

He was a gentle man, but masculine with a defined jawline; tall and well-built for a man of his age. Very deep voice, macho, but something about him gives off the impression that he has a sensitive nature, and is very caring and respectful of others. As an African-

American man who has endured many acts of racism while living and working in the "Democratic" blue-collared city of Chicago, because of those negative occurrences, I'm somewhat befuddled by my positive impression of this elderly white man.

"SIXTY-TWO YEARS", I exclaimed!

"WOWWWW!!! Same wife; same husband?" I pointed to the mature lady cuddling with him to get her to affirm what I was asking.

"Yes", as she nodded her head and smiled.

Her name was Elizabeth, and what captured my attention were her charming smile and the afterglow of the sunset beaming from her eyes. The comforting look upon her face gave me the perception that her gentle spirit is probably the reason why her husband is in tune with his sensitive nature, caring, and respectful of others. There was an aura of joy and happiness that appeared to ooze out of them both. I could feel their vibrations, and was immediately lifted to a higher emotional state.

"I'm curious, and of course you're probably asked this often, what's the secret to your long marriage? You seem so merry and at peace with one another!"

"Well young man I'll share a short story with you. Our marriage wasn't always as happy as it has been for the past fifty years. When I was your age I was a workaholic and not the best husband. I valued my career more than I appreciated my wife and family. Often after work I would join a few coworkers for Happy Hour; while we sat at the bar and after a few cocktails most of the men would begin complaining about their wives and children. And after we would sober up, the fellas would jokingly say, "Well I guess it's time for me to go home and talk to my wife and play with my kids.

But they all seemed so unhappy and pathetic with this routine. However, I liked and was fond of my wife and children, but couldn't understand why she and I would fight a lot when I came home. And as I sat there silently analyzing my friend's relationships, I realized what was wrong in mine, and made the decision right then and there to change and improve my marriage.

*Like success, misery also leaves clues, young man. My friends who were living 'unhappily ever after' are going home to 'talk with their wives and play with their kids'. So I decided from henceforth to do the opposite. I'm going home to 'talk to my kids and **PLAY WITH MY WIFE!'***

The two of them laughed hysterically as if he had told this parable a million times, but the story never gets old to them. I couldn't help but laugh heartily also.

"Young Man, a happy wife is a requirement for a happy life. But to have a happy wife after all these years you must continue to treat your wife like she is the woman whom you hope to someday marry."

I sat back for a moment to immerse in this newfound knowledge and insight.

"Sir, that is a powerful piece of advice. Treat your wife like she is the woman that you hope to someday marry."

"And also young man", the elderly woman said to me; *"your wife should always present herself to you as the woman you will want to stay in a marriage with".*

I was in awe. I remained in silence, sitting next to them on the bench, gazing out at the lake, and basking in their euphoric energy. I felt like I was having a metaphysical occurrence; it was divine. In that moment my heart was opened, and my mindset about marriage had been renewed. I came to accept that perhaps marriage is *NOT* hard work. *However, being married to someone you don't like is **very** hard.*

Every marriage begins on a high vibration, most likely at its highest emotional state. The two of you are excited. The adventures of your lifetime together earnestly await your arrival. And then someone or perhaps multiple people begin to convince you that "marriage is hard work". Suddenly you start believing that you and your spouse can't be this happy all the time; unintentionally you begin to look for reasons and scenarios to prove that *marriage is not easy* and that there will always be stomach churning ups and downs or heart wrenching challenges in your matrimony. And I do not pretend that you won't face confrontations and disagreements throughout your lifespan together. But surely there must be a difference between "facing challenges while married" versus "challenges that affect your marriage".

Infatuation. Passion. Lust. In the beginning everything is exhilarating. You're in the midst of wedded bliss and enjoying each other's energy, love, and intimacy, all the while expecting something awful to happen because you've been told that it would and you have also witnessed this happening with other couples. As time passes you unwittingly start asking, *"Why aren't we fighting like most couples?"; "we've been married for a month, year or two, something bad should be happening"*. You become confused by how well things are going for you and your mate.

But have you noticed that no one ever says that about *friendships*? Has it ever been brought to your attention by someone saying, *"Friendships are hard work"*? But isn't a friendship a relationship much like a marriage, (without sex, children together, and shared financial responsibilities, of course). So, in most cases why isn't being someone's best friend **hard** for you or them? Because we *LIKE* our friends.

We develop friendships with people that are just like us. And for most people, we actually like ourselves and believe that we are a great friend. We attract friends that are compatible and have similar tastes, ideas, and philosophies. We enjoy their company, and even when we disagree we find a reason to compromise, forgive, rebuild and continue the friendship for decades. Many people have friendships that have outlasted multiple relationships and marriages. The primary reason for this is that subconsciously we don't feel that *friendships are laborious.*

However, embedded in the universal psyche of humanity we believe that being in a marriage will somehow attract major obstacles, and that our union will be tested by issues that could negatively impact our future together. And although we intuitively believe this, we as humans still desire to be married. Seems strange, but there has to be a reason why.

Consciously or unknowingly, negative thoughts about marriage will create an emotional reaction in your spirit (*your soul, your vibrational vortex*). My friends Al and his wife Sharon relationship is a great example of this.

Thoughts and emotions, left unchecked, will eventually create a physical response. These three occurrences when are acted out consecutively (*thoughts, emotions, and physical responses*) will cause you to spiritually and physically attract to you what you've been giving your attention. Whether good or bad, whatever you give continuous acknowledgement, left unrestrained, will eventually manifest in your life.

Chapter 3:

Unhappily, but we're STILL together

Al and Sharon

"'To forsake all others has fallen on deaf ears.' I know this bitch is cheating on me. It's damn near midnight and she's still not home. Ain't no fucking way that she's still with her clients, and she's not answering her phone; Al says to himself as he reaches for his iPhone to text his wife for what feels like the 100th time.

"Where the FUCK are you, Sharon?" he texts with an angry face emoji.

As a partner with the largest marketing and advertising agency in Atlanta, it is not uncommon for his wife to work late into the night. Still he is anxious; blood in his veins boiling; and sweating profusely. His mind inundated with visions of her being unfaithful. But three hours' prior, her safety was his primary concern when she wasn't home at her usual 6:30pm arrival time.

Alan Johnson, affectionately known by his friends as Al, is a manager for the Department of Public Works for the city of Atlanta. He has always been intimidated by his wife's high profile position.

Sharon is a well-toned curvy woman adorn with long legs that makes her look taller than her 5'4" frame. Having great pride in her appearance she is incessant with her daily exercise routines and very seldom eats anything that will compromise her fitness goals. Throughout her entire life she has been recognized by many for her physical beauty; in the corporate world she's even more recognized because of her academic accomplishments and the success she enjoys in her career.

Smart, beautiful, and a go-getter; all of the attributes that Al always wanted in a woman, but has continuously felt that his wife was out of his league. And even though he has what many working class Americans would consider a "good paying job" earning over $85,000 annually, he's even more intimidated that his wife earns five times as much. Standing 5'9", the extra 47 pounds he's gained over the years has dwarfed his confidence.

Alan and Sharon dated during their last two years at Howard University. Many of Sharon's friends were shocked when they started dating because he was completely different than the guys she normally went out with. But her commitment to graduating with honors and involvement in many social clubs on campus, oftentimes she had to remind her friends that she needed to date someone who would not be a distraction to her goals. Sharon liked Al because he was smart and made her laugh; she felt safe with him. And even though he knew that he was the "safe guy" and not her "fantasy guy", he didn't let it bother him because he was in a relationship with the hottest girl on campus. He gloated in this accomplishment.

Alan and Sharon married shortly after graduating college eleven years ago and have created for themselves and their 4-year-old daughter Ashley an accomplished and very comfortable lifestyle in the Atlanta suburb of Marietta, Georgia. Yet while enjoying "high society", because of his insecurities, Al always finds a way to add gloom into their way of life. As an outlet to escape her husband's jealousy, self-doubts, and arguments, Sharon tends to bury herself into her work and from time to time may work long hours at the office.

"Daddy where's Mommy", their 4-year-old daughter Ashley asks with a little sad face that always garner immediate attention from her beloved dad.

"Mommy will be home soon sweetheart; it's almost 8 o'clock; let's get you ready for bed".

"But Daddy I want Mommy!"

"I know sweetheart. Mommy will be home soon to kiss you good night like she always does. Come, let Daddy tuck you in and we'll say our prayers."

Al has been texting and calling Sharon for two hours and still no response. Even worse is that when he called her phone at 8:17pm, the call was answered but no one said anything.

"Hello! Hello! Sharon?" Nothing.

He grabs the remote control off of the table, points it at the television to mute the volume, while standing in the center of their family room; he held his cell phone firmly to his left ear and closed his eyes to listen without any distractions. He is convinced that he can hear murmurs, romantic sounds and excessive breathing in the background. Uncertain if he has heard his wife's voice, yet he becomes more fanatical, his mind races with thoughts of infidelity. To avoid further distractions from his daughter Ashley, he rushes through their usual nightly routine. But while laying across her bed and rocking her in his arms, Al falls into a lucid dream of his wife being kissed by another man. Becoming distraught and seething from the mental images of her in full ecstasy and enjoying the touch of one of her coworkers. Conscious that he is dreaming he tries to see the face of the man engaged in lascivious acts with Robin; even asking himself questions to draw a clearer picture. He sketches him as tall with an athletic build, dark and handsome like the guys his wife trains with at the gym. Every mental portrait he creates paints himself into a deeper state of anguish. He finally conceives that he knows who Sharon's lover may be.

Quickly sitting up on the bed Al blurts out *"I knew she liked that motherfucker. I felt it!"*

On multiple occasions when visiting her workplace or attending a company event he shared with me that he could feel that she may have had an attraction to this one guy in particular, but I dismissed it as foolish jealousy.

Spencer McArthur, senior Vice President of Marketing. Sharon and Spencer have worked together for almost five years. Although radical, for Al to ease his mind from believing that Spencer is someone that his wife may be attracted to, he usually dismisses the thought because Spencer is also married without a prenuptial and with children. He concludes that the risks for Spencer are too great. And that he has a lot to lose if he's ever caught having an affair.

"Holy shit, wait! Al screams as he awakens from this dream-state. Thoughts racing across his mind at lightning speed. Quietly and slowly he removes Ashley off of his chest, gently placing her on the bed to keep from waking her up. Walking back into the family room he thinks "o fuck, as *a married man who would be better to have an affair with other than a married woman who also has a lot to lose".*

Clinching his fist and speaking out loud, *"I swear to God she better not be screwing around on me."*

After calling her phone and getting Sharon's voicemail again, still standing in the middle of the room with his cellphone firmly pressed against his ear and screaming into the phone again, giving no consideration that he could be awakening his young daughter who's sleeping in the bedroom just above the family room.

"HELLO!"

"SHARON!"

"HELLO", he continues to yell, all to no avail.

For forty-eight seconds he listens intently for more proof of her betrayal but the pounding sounds of his racing heartbeat drowns out the illicit relations that he thinks he's hearing.

Suddenly the call ends. He looks at his phone. Shaking and panicking he calls her phone again and again with no luck. He paces throughout the house, trying not to be too loud that Ashley wakes up. He can't simultaneously handle being a *"doting father"* while anger towards the mother of his child is eating away at his heart and soul.

"ANSWER YOUR FUCKING PHONE!"; he texts again.

"WHERE ARE YOU AND WHO ARE YOU WITH!"

"I CALLED YOU. You better call me back RIGHT NOW!!!"

Thirty-four text messages and multiple voicemails until her voicemail became full. Al is livid. His body becomes nauseated because of his explicit imagination.

He envisions her laying across the expensive Mahogany Brookhaven desk with her right leg draped across his left shoulder while Spencer gently begins to kiss the inside of Sharon's legs, and then moves his tongue across her right inner thigh.

Enraged and entranced by the illicit images running rampantly across his neocortex he again speaks out loud:

"Yeah that bitch likes that shit".

He's reminded of their first rendezvous and her reactions when they first made love.

He sees Spencer strong hands gripping her succulent breasts continuously while he seals his affection with a kiss upon her every *erogenous zone*. The heat and the erotic scent pulsating out her *love canal* have awakened an intense craving within Spencer and he cannot wait to place himself inside of her. He teases her just a little while longer, but Sharon is on to his attempts to make her body beg for him. As an alpha female she sits up on the desk and pushes him off of her and into her costly Stanford Executive desk chair. She kneels down in front him, the gaze in her eyes inflamed with a fire of passion as she stares deeply into Spencer's soul, and with her mouth she *reciprocates the pleasure* that he had moments earlier given to her.

Al is at home going bonkers. Each one of the images in his head and with the alcohol raging in his veins makes the thoughts of his wife-cheating feel even more real. Every enjoyment that Spencer has with Al's bride, he sensationalizes. Every exhale that Sharon breathes Al can feel upon his own face. Their kisses he tastes, and the aroma of their lovemaking he can smell. Moments away from a mental breakdown, he is roused suddenly from this X-rated nightmare to the sound of the garage door opening which confirms that Sharon is finally home.

His white button down work shirt that he wears so proudly with **Alan Johnson** engraved on the left and his title of **Solid Waste Code Enforcement Officer** stitched just above the right pocket is drenched from him sweating profusely. Al rushes into the bathroom across from the kitchen for a towel to wipe his face and collect himself before his wife comes inside. Staring in the mirror while frantically trying to compose himself Al is perplexed by his emotions, he doesn't know if he's angry or happy that Sharon has made it home safely. But he knows that he wants some answers, and the look of exhaustion from a long arduous workday on her face reveals that she hasn't been cheating. However, he suffered the consequences of his thoughts equally as much as he would have if he had actual proof of any extramarital relations.

Our thoughts, real or imagine, create our reality. So whatever you don't want to experience in your marriage, think, feel, and speak only the good that you desire to enjoy instead. Instead of visualizing Sharon with another man, Al's fantasies would have been a lot more erotic if he had fancied himself as her *other man*; something that my ex-wife's friend Tiana knows how to do all too well.

CHAPTER 4:
"Great Sex and Good Health"
Ryan and Tiana

"Hey babe, do we have any plans for tonight?" While at work Ryan called his wife to invite her out for a much needed date night. Life in the Anderson home has been intense because of all of the demands with raising three children (ages 13, 10, and 7); constantly running errands after work and never-ending chores around the house; and some minor medical issues that Ryan has been suffering from over the past year and a half.

"Do we ever have plans?", his wife Tiana, whom he's been married to for 16 years, replies with a bit of frustration in her tone.

No one can blame her for how she's been feeling lately. The incessant demands as a Senior Administrative Assistant at a large accounting firm located downtown Chicago; volunteering for their daughter's Girl Scout troop; and chaperoning their oldest son and two of his teammates to and from swim practices and meets each weekend has Tiana feeling beaten and worn. And the lack of intimacy that have plagued their sex life over the past three months really has her on edge. Everyone in their home tiptoes around to keep from upsetting mom. And although she knows that home life for the Anderson's has not been as jovial as they used to be, she is cautious of her actions and makes previsions to keep from looking stressed out and responding to her family irrationally.

"Tony and Nicole invited us to dinner and a comedy show tonight. I thought it would be fun since Nelsen doesn't have a swim meet nor practice tomorrow, selling Girl Scout cookies for Brianna has ended, and my mom has agreed to babysit Nadia. We can finally sleep in, and maybe when we get home from the club tonight we can do a little something-something", Ryan says with a mannish smirk on his face and romantic humor in his voice.

"You know what, I can use a night out. Yeah let's do it", Tiana says.

Ryan, Tiana, Tony, and Nicole all come together at a popular Mexican restaurant for dinner and drinks. Within the first half hour Tiana notices that Ryan has already drunk two Martinis and just requested a third, and the meals that they each have ordered have not arrived yet. She privately taps his thigh underneath the table as a hint to take it easy on the drinks.

Leaning closer to whisper in his ear, *"Ryan, do me a favor and slow down on the alcohol; you remember what happened the last time you had too much to drink. I really want to make love tonight. I'm frustrated and I am horny. I need to be fucked."*

"Don't worry baby, I got you. I still have one blue pill left from my prescription. It's on tonight baby." He winks at her as his confidence rises with each sip of his third Martini. But Tiana is not so convinced, and despite her lack of confidence in how the night will end she decides to continue having fun anyway.

She glances across the table at Tony and Nicole in admiration.

"Nicole is so gorgeous, so pretty", she thinks how even in high school she was the girl that every guy wanted and all other girls wanted to look like. *"And her dress looks great on her body!"* Tiana reflects on how when Nicole and Tony started dating all of her friends marveled at their amazing relationship and was hypnotized when she shared stories of their intimacy.

And for a fleeting moment Tianna is reminded of she and Ryan's past sex life and how wonderful it used to be, and yearns for those *good-ole-days* to return. She continues thinking about Tony and Nicole, but with each thought of their deep admiration for each other and how physically captivating they are, she becomes even angrier and disappointed at Ryan for allowing himself to get so horribly out of shape.

"Excuse me waiter, may I have another glass of Merlot."

Tianna drinks the glass of her favorite wine to suppress the discontentment that's trying to creep into her heart for her husband, and the lustful thoughts she's having of Tony making love to Nicole. For a brief moment she's starting to see herself as Nicole. She doesn't want to be her nor does she want to have sex with Tony, but she can't help but think of how exciting it would be to trade places with them, at least for one night. *Tonight,* if it were possible.

"Hey guys, let's get the bill and head over to the Laughing Gas. That fool Marquis Jones is going to have the audience cracking the fuck up. He's straight up ig'nant"; Tony says. They all laughed in agreement.

"But what I like about him the most is that he keeps it real, and says what we all really want to say but won't", said Ryan. The laughter continues.

They finally get to their seats after waiting in line for almost an hour. Ryan orders a round of beers for him and Tony and two *Cosmopolitans* for the ladies. Tiana protested at first but didn't want to seem like she wasn't having a good time in front of their friends.

"Baby, I'm so serious I need to be fucked tonight"; she firmly looks into his eyes as the Host comes on stage to start the show.

"Welcome to the Laughing Gas y'all; tonight's show is going to be hilarious and off the chain. Are y'all ready to have a good time?" The crowd roars in excitement. He introduces the first two comedians before bringing out the headliner, Marquis Jones. Although the two previous acts weren't as funny as the audience had anticipated, the energy between Tiana and Ryan was no laughing matter either.

With each serving of drinks that Ryan orders, Tiana's desire for sex with her husband waned. She starts to look at him with disgust. She loves him dearly and is still in love with him, but their lack of sexual affection over the past year is causing resentment in their marriage. She secretly watches porn and pleasures herself often when Ryan is not around. As the host is reading Marquis Jones's bio she glanced over at Tony.

"Look how his blazer is tapered so well against his arms and chest; and he smells enticing. I wonder what's the name of the cologne he is wearing."

She finds herself entranced in a raunchy scene from an adult-rated movie that Ryan is unaware she watches on her password protected iPad when she is bathing in their giant soaking tub. She holds the iPad in her left hand as her right hand slowly rubs across her breast and glides down her stomach and then into the searing bubble bath she has drawn for herself. She lays the iPad on the small table next to the tub and gives permission to her left hand to join the right as she continues to gratify herself.

"May I get you anything else", the waitress asked Tiana. She is startled by the waitress's voice and is pulled out of her trance as she rejoins the rest of the audience who are thoroughly enjoying the comedy show.

"By show of hands, how many married couples are here tonight", comedian Marquis asked the audience.

"I love it! You know my wife and I have been together for almost 20 years now." The audience applauds.

"It hasn't always been easy. Y'all know how it is. The older you get shit starts to change. Now I can handle all of the

changes with kids, jobs, friends and shit. But the biggest change is that I'm an old muhfucka now.

DAMN! Getting older sucks!"

The audience laughs and applauds in agreement.

"And I didn't realize how much television would still have a huge influence on my relationship. My wife and I went to college because of the show "A Different World". We got married because of the characters Dwayne and Whitley. And last year my fat ass started going to the gym because of the character Ghost from the hit Showtime cable drama series POWER! WHAT THE FUCK MAN!

Loud applauds and screams erupted from the females in the audience.

"This good looking muhfucka has women all around the world wishing that their nigga...looked like that nigga. A regular nigga with a physique like mines can't compete with him."

The audience is cracking up, and all of the ladies are cheering continuously.

"Fellas, am I lying? How many of you, while watching the show, glanced at your lady while Ghost was fucking the shit out of Angela, and saw your woman salivating and

staring at the television with a look on her face like daaaamnnnn I wish that I was Angela right now!"

Everyone is laughing hysterically, including Tiana and Ryan.

*"And what's fucked up y'all is that she isn't wishing that you looked like Ghost; her ass is wishing that she were being **fucked** by Ghost! Every regular nigga in America was glad when Tariq killed his monkey ass. I was like YES; kill that pretty Ricky looking ass muthafucka! LOL!"*

Marquis couldn't help but to laugh out loud also.

"I'm just playing y'all! But seriously, it's not popular to say but the truth is NO woman fantasizes about being "broke off" by a fat guy. Not even an overweight woman dreams of having sex with an overweight man. This fat muhfucka has diabetes and high blood pressure. His dick can't get hard and shit. That isn't her fantasy. Hell, she may even have high blood pressure and diabetes, but the nigga in her fantasy is ripped, chiseled, tall, dark, and handsome with a big dick."

Everyone is laughing and cheering; even some women are standing in their chairs waving their white dinner cloth in the air with agreement of what Marquis is saying. But Ryan is starting to feel really bad, and no longer feeling the buzz from his drinks. These jokes are starting to hit home.

"Her fantasy guy is slim and fit, and can give her long deep strokes for hours. Even if the muthafucka cum quickly she knows his dick will rise again in about 10-15 minutes. The muthafucka even has "STILL I RISE" tattooed on his dick."

Tiana and Nicole are in tears from laughing so hard. The two of them are having fun, but Ryan isn't. He and Tony look at each other, and embarrassment can be seen written all over Ryan's face.

"In 15 minutes, her fantasy guy will be readily available to lay into that ass for at least another 45 minute straight. But yo fat ass need at least 48-72 hours before you can hit again; cause it's going to take 2-3 days to digest all the unhealthy shit you've been eating and drinking all damn day.

I had to get my ass in THE GYM; Marquis exclaims loudly. *Fuuuuuck that being fat and out of shape shit! Ain't no nigga going to be long stroking my wife. Fuck that!*

I also hired a nutritionist so I can learn about foods that give me stamina. Even my female nutritionist taught me that women not only want a guy who can give her long strokes, but she also wants to be made love to. She expressed that *"yeah we love being fuck hard, long, and strong as he's making love to our minds and saying romantic shit while we're having sex."*

All of the women clapped in agreement.

"You can't do that when you can barely hold your big ass up, and sweat pouring down your face, breathing all heavy while on top of her. That shit ain't romantic! You don't ever see that kind of erotic scenes in cinema, regular movies or porn movies. Ain't shit sexy about a fat guy!

Fellas, when she says that she wants a guy that's "thick with a lot of girth", Bro, she's talking about your penis...not your waistline muthafucka!"

Tony almost spits out his drink while laughing so hard. Nicole and Tiana are holding each other, giggling and snickering like two high school teenagers at a sleepover, and agreeing with everything Marquis is saying.

"Girl he is telling the truth. He is straight...keeping it real", as they point to each other in unison.

But Ryan is the only one who's not amused.

Fellas, you can't hit dat shit long and deep with a chick with a 'phat ass', and yo fat ass stomach is lying on top of her ass. Come on man; let's keep it real.

For the rest of the show Ryan was silent and everything around him faded to black, including their drive back home. That night, Ryan didn't attempt to make love to Tiana, nor was she expecting it. As usual he fell asleep on the sofa while Tiana, like my brother Michael, scrolled through her social media accounts, entertaining herself in their soaking tub with her iPad in her left hand and her right hand inside of her steamy scorching bubble bath.

Chapter 5
Social Media:
Michael and LaTonya

Barely a glimpse of the sun ascending over the horizon, he's already awake, and his first thoughts are of her. As he does each morning he reaches across to grab her. He loves the feel of her in his hands; slim, firm, her dark black skin tone so tightly encased. Built by Apple, the glow from his iPhone is majestic, spellbinding, he can't stop staring at her. A smile creeps upon his countenance as he slowly scrolls his fingers across her face. He's enraptured by thoughts of how she makes him feel. He gets everything he wants from her, like a genie, except with her, the wishes are endless.

So many imperfections in the outside world, but with one push of his thumb upon one of her many apps he joins a world where everything is tranquil.

My brother Michael and his wife LaTonya have been married for seventeen years. For Michael, life as a married man has begun to feel ordinary and ritual. For adventure he seeks out stimulation from his "side chick". Her name is *Social Media*, and she makes everything look desirable, she motivates him, gives him a sense of security. He lets her control his mind, his actions, his emotions, and his entire being in general. For Michael, like candy is to a child, Social Media is addictive.

Michael enjoys role playing with her; she's goes by many names to satisfy his fantasies. When he's with *Instagram* he's constantly smiling. Often you may hear him mumbling, *"she's so beautiful"* as she models different high-end clothing. But he especially likes when she's scantily clad in string bikinis or just a tiny bra and thong while parading around for his illusions. He admires everything about this *woman* and no human being can take her place. Her body is impeccable; one that even cosmetic surgeons admire. He endures hours gawking at her, she's ageless and her beauty never fades; his wish is that their relationship would last forever.

Beyond her physical attributes *Instagram* takes him to exotic vacation destinations he has never traveled to, creating visual memories so real that he was able to articulate to people very well, making them believe that they were the best vacations he has ever experienced. Since their relationship began four years ago Michael and Instagram have been on world adventures and reached exotic vacations in the blink of an eye, each destination even more enchanting.

He loves that she is not ashamed of their relationship; posting pictures of them side-by-side while dining at five-star restaurants. Even their home cooked meals look prepared by a renowned chef. His favorite posts are of the two of them toasting to a $1500 bottle of *VEUVE CLICQUOT Yellow Label Brut Champagne* or drinking glasses of their favorite *JUSTIN ISOSCELES Cabernet Sauvignon* and watching breathtaking sunsets, their romance seems picturesque.

For short romances and a secret rendezvous he turns to *Tinder*; Michael is drawn to her because she's young, vibrant, and affectionate. Her playful and youthful personality makes him feel spirited. She doesn't want much from a man his age, but what she does want he can provide. He's okay with being used as her sugar daddy because she enjoys the attention he gives to her that a man her age isn't mature enough to grant. Tinder makes Michael feel the way his wife no longer does.

When Michael and LaTonya's relationship began her creativity was exciting and the satisfaction she brought was unmatched, but those days are long gone. Their nights together were once amorous, erotic, passionate. Thoughtful gifts were constant, and she made him feel loved and appreciated, and that he was the perfect man for her. She would tell him fantastic stories to lift his mood, awaken the spirit of adventure deep within him, and made him want to try new things. Somehow the two of them have allowed monotony to creep into their marriage and now their relationship feels stale. All of the attributes that once existed in their marriage he now has instant access to through hundreds of apps on his cellphone. His iPhone is likening to a very understanding woman, does not stress him for anything, and lets him do whatever he wants that makes him happy. When he's troubled, she offers a soothing voice that answers to his every command.

Also, Michael has been dating *Facebook* a very long time because she understands that he may need to stay in touch with a past lover or two, catch up and check up on them, maybe even meet up every so often. Facebook never faults him because she loves him and never wants to see him unhappy or lacking anything.

He wonders as he keeps staring at her, admiring her more and more, always finding a new thing to add to the list of the many reasons why he loves her so much. He doesn't even notice just how fast the time has flown by, as his thoughts and senses are completely engrossed in this "woman". The real world around him at this point is blank and silent, and his attention to his family is none.

But just like his marriage with LaTonya, Michael constantly compares FB (as he affectionately refers to her) to all the other apps available to him, and the differences are all too clear. But the nagging, the incessant appeals for his attention, the insatiable need to *talk* while he's at work, at the gym, or driving home, and the endless demand for accountability, they are all too much for him. He feels like a caged animal. He cannot do whatever he feels makes him happy because he always has to explain himself. He is constantly needed to keep giving more of himself and this relationship with Facebook emotionally draining him.

Hours later, it's now time to start doing other things, very quickly, so he can go back to being with his *Social Media*. So he gets up from the bed and heads straight for the bathroom. He looks into the mirror and for a second, he can feel heavy loneliness in his heart. He feels empty like there is a deep consuming hole inside him that he does not know how to fill. His endless thoughts are torturous and shear hopelessness and depression takes over him completely, it's almost unbearable.

However, he recognizes this feeling. It's not the first time, nor the second; it's always there, every single day, especially when he has accidentally left or lost his phone. Away from her, he does not sense love, or feel supported by his wife, nor does he know how to appreciate the wonderful life that he has. He has centered his world around *Social Media*, his happiness depends on her, his view of life is built upon how she presents it to him, and so without her, he feels incomplete.

He's now staring at the face looking at him in the mirror, and he cannot tell who he is. Because of Snapchat filters, photo shopped pics, and cropped images his identity has been distorted, he's high on a type of drug with the worst withdrawal symptoms. If only he could stop, but does he want to end this affair? Could he give up the false security she has given him? Is he ready to face the world he had completely shut down for her? Does he even remember what this world was like before he met *Social Media*? *"It's not worth it,"* he says to himself, and with that, he takes a quick shower and goes back to the bedroom.

He stands at the far corner of the bed and looks at the female sleeping on it. The woman he calls his wife. Someone that has become a stranger to him over the years. She's completely covered up that only her hair is exposed, and she's facing the wall. He tries to imagine her face in his mind and he can't seem to figure it out.

"Does she have dimples? Are her lips pink or dark? Does she have freckles and is she petite or plump?" None of these details rang a bell in his mind, after all, when was the last time he had an actual conversation with her or looked at her square in the face? He was too busy with his *other women* to take notice of the one who deserves all of his attention, his wife.

His eyes wander off to the framed pictures on the bedside table. One was of his five kids and they looked beautiful. They were smiling and looked very happy, they were quite young in the photo. The rest of the pictures were of his wife and the kids in different places and in various stages of their lives. There was one photo taken a short time ago of the family laughing on a rollercoaster and he couldn't help but smile. Then a thought struck him, why was he not on that picture? In fact, why was he not on any of the pictures? For a brief moment the thinks to himself that his side chick has much prettier pictures anyway, so whatever, he couldn't care less. He doesn't give it much thought anymore.

He casually walks towards his dresser to get dressed and leave. As he's putting on his shoes, he can hear his wife turning over behind him and was saying something he didn't listen to. He was in too much of a hurry to get to his favorite woman, *Social Media*. He gets up, looks at his wife looking at him waiting for an answer, and walks away, he after all had no answer to give because he had heard nothing she said and didn't want to wait another moment to give her enough time to repeat it.

Once he is out of the house and in the office, he turns to *Instagram* again. He's happy and relaxed, and with his phone in his hand he tunes out the real world that actually matters, to temporarily enjoy the ever sweet company that the countless imaginary women that Social Media makes so easily available to him.

A lot of people do not notice just how much they let social media control them. Like Michael, social media shows them things they wish they had and allows them to expand their imagination. However, it may also misdirect you into disconnecting with reality.

Without his cellphone and endless apps Michael felt empty and lonely when he wasn't scrolling through social media. This is because he now had to face what was going on around him and it was nothing close to the perfection he saw online which depressed him. He had turned away from his family and put his marriage in jeopardy.

He was as much a stranger to himself as he was to those around him. He didn't even care to know what his wife was saying. He was doing whatever he wanted and didn't concern himself about the effects it all had on his actual life. Michael humiliates his wife, disrespects her, makes her feel unloved and unwanted and even worse, cheating on her and having intimate conversations with past lovers. But infidelity is not always physical intercourse with a person outside of your marriage. It's also withholding attention from your significant other to give that attention to your fantasies. He has no emotional connection to my sister-in-law or their children. This marriage is already dead.

It is imperative to remember that in most scenarios what we see on social media is an illusion. Very few people post the ugly side of their relationship or lifestyle. Be wise enough to choose how what you see affects you and those around you. And every so often logoff, unplug and disconnect from virtual reality, and spend that time enjoying the real world.

LaTonya Shares Her Story

"Glancing down at the clock in the bottom right side of my computer and I cannot believe that it's only 4:49pm; the last 30 minutes of my workday always feel like hours. I am tired and just want to get home and relax before another tiring day at the office tomorrow. I quickly pack up my work desk and get ready to leave.

As I arrange my desk I see a picture of my family which has been here ever since I started this job twelve years ago. My husband and our children were on it, smiling, looking as happy as ever. And we were cheerful, the good old times which now felt like a lifetime ago. I could feel a sudden surge of anger rush through me. 'My husband', I say in disgust. The source of my misery in recent years. Walking through the parking garage towards my car I think to myself why was I still married to him anyway? I wasn't happy with him anymore. He's not the man I would rather be with. He is nothing like other husbands. He has failed me as a mate and is a disappointment to our children. I could feel hate slowly creeping up my throat and choking me and I let out a loud gasp.

Arriving home an hour later I see his car parked in the driveway, as usual. Travel time home is normally a 30 minutes' drive from my work on a good day, but with the traffic on this particular day, I was lucky to make it home as quickly as I did. So while sitting in my car, stuck in stationary traffic listening to some smooth John Legend as my mind wanders off to something I saw earlier today.

I was looking through my Instagram, as usual, and I saw the cutest video. This girl had posted a video of a surprise her boyfriend had prepared for her and it was the most romantic thing in the world. He had decorated their living room with red roses all around the chandelier, the walls were dressed up with stripes of bright white Christmas lights. The furniture had been moved to leave a large space in the center where there was a white rug surrounded by red candles. At the heart of the rug was a basket full of different types of chocolate, some cakes, a bottle of wine, and more roses in the middle of the basket. Then around the basket were different kinds of food. There was chicken, pizza, guacamole, fish, pasta, and more wine with the cutest glasses on each side of the bottle. The moment she opened the door, the boyfriend handed her a single rose, kissed her, and proceeded to film her reaction. According to her caption, it wasn't any special occasion, it was just a normal night and he was feeling nostalgic.

Why can't I have that? Why can't Michael awaken one day and decide to surprise me like that or any other way whatsoever? All he knew was taking me to restaurants once in a while to just eat things we can make at home instead of wasting money. The guy I saw on Instagram was just her boyfriend and he was going all out, making his girlfriend the focus of his world and my husband couldn't even look at me for five minutes. And there again I can feel a huge lump in my throat.

The traffic was moving now so I start my engine and carefully follow the car in front of me. When we stop again, my mind goes back to that video, and several others I watched after that. Girls out here were being treated like queens and they were not even married yet and I struggle to remember the last time my husband stood a few feet close to me, why was I so unlucky? Can I switch husbands with some of these girls for just a day, please? The girls I saw were getting expensive gifts and being taken to trips around the world, they were taking perfect pictures and they seemed to have an ideal relationship. It's like they lived on a planet I was not aware of. They say that men are from Mars and women are from Venus, but these ladies have seemed to attract men from Mars with the heart of a woman; it's like they know exactly what a female desire without her having to say it repeatedly. I am so tempted to reactivate my dating profile on Plenty of Fish. I just want to feel wanted again; to feel pretty and sexy. Vibrant. Youthful.

After parking my car next to Michael's I was overcome by a feeling of dread. Do I have to go in? Can he just disappear from my life and be replaced with someone I deserve? I'm already in a foul mood before walking in. I open the door and there he is. Walking around without a shirt on like he owned the world. "Hey Tonya," he says. Even his voice made me annoyed. I could only afford a low, "mm," in response. I wanted to be away from him.

I look around, the house is clean and ...." mommy! Mommy! You're home!" My son cries almost tackling me to the ground, and for those few minutes, I find my smile again. Our youngest child is eight years old and is always the highlight of my days and as I tightly hug him back, my heart is at peace again, until the husband walks by. Looking at his hanging belly, hairy chest, and ungroomed beard, I couldn't help but feel grossed out. The men I see on Plenty of Fish and Match.com clearly know their way to the gym. They have chiseled abs and toned bodies and clean chests. Their beards are well shaved and neat and you can almost smell the cologne they're wearing through the pictures. I'm no Instagram fitness model but I work out tirelessly to look good and this man is here living his best life looking like a caveman! Damn.

I slowly rise from where I was kneeling with my son and walk into the kitchen. There was a pot on the stove and upon opening it, I see some unappealing pasta in some flat sauce and I just want to die. Can't this man do anything right? There are couples all over social media cooking together as they throw flour at each other as they giggle and make out. Other women get home and find the husbands have made a five-course meal to die for but this is what I come home to? Why?

I'm furious at this point so I grumpily walk straight to my bedroom. The bed, of course, wasn't even made straight. "If you can't make the bed properly then don't make it all!" I shout. I take off my clothes, take a quick bath, and get into bed, I didn't even want the wine anymore.

I was too frustrated to fall asleep so I kept tossing and turning. After a while, I felt my husband come into the room and get into bed. He tries to hold me but I push him away, he puts his hand on my shoulder to get my attention but I shrug it off. In a scared low voice, he says, "can we please talk?" Of course, he can't even speak like a man either, no authority in his voice, this is a nightmare, I think to myself, I need a man more like the ones I see on social media.

I pull the blankets over my face and completely ignore him. I close my eyes and silently hope he doesn't speak again. I can't stand that irritating voice. I just hope this night ends soon, so I can go to work and be away from him.

Some people may think that LaTonya is completely delusional for allowing social media to affect how she views her marriage. She no longer respects her husband and has disconnected herself from him. However, this may have happened as a result of the amount of time that Michael spends with social media. They both are guilty of not realizing that what is seen on social media is a fraction of a 24-hour time span. Often, people fake a lot of situations to look perfect.

LaTonya has allowed herself to no longer appreciate the little things her husband does. Yes, the food was not perfect, but it's important to show gratitude that he made the effort, same as with making of the bed or cleaning the house. Expensive and elaborate surprises are nice, but quality time together in any scenario is lovelier, and even more important.

I learned from a friend and Life Coach that LaTonya does not realize that she is contributing to the demise of her marriage especially when she talks about needing a new man. He said that when a couple marry they become one heart, one mind, one spirit. What one feels the other can experience also. Thoughts of infidelity, though you think are private, are creating a vibrational energy that your spouse can sense. Words may not be said, but every couple can feel when something is off in their relationship. That means she is slowly inclining towards infidelity, and that would be the final nail in the coffin. She has pushed my brother Michael away so often that he is now afraid of talking to her, he no longer feels safe approaching her which is a scary situation for the two of them. To have a successful marriage, feeling emotionally secure and free to express yourself with one another is critical.

Social media doesn't have to be a bad thing; it can also be a very useful tool. Instead of the two of them acting the way they have been, they should be using what they see on these social outlets as an inspiration for things they could do for each other to add joy to their marriage, and a feeling of love, appreciation, and adoration for their relationship, feelings that will bring them closer to living happily ever after.

But in order to achieve this couples must disconnect from the virtual world and from giving so much attention to things that please you physically, and reconnect to the internal beauty and benefits of a marriage and the things that connects us spiritually, and ideology and sacred practices that my sister Shanice learned from her friend Adrianna after they attended a single and divorce retreat last summer.

"Nature's Beauty"
A poem dedicated to God's Creation

"I drink the rays of Her sunshine
...and bathe in the washing of Her Word
I want to hold God's hand and lead Her through the green pastures
...and show Her the colorful lilies of the fields.

I want to stroll with Her along the still waters of the Divine River of Love,
...as I sing Her passages from the *Song of Songs*
I want to dance with Her to the rhythms from the Symphony of David
...as we glide across the floor to the beat of Her heart.

O how I yearn to gaze into Her eyes and see the beauty of Her creation
....as I honor Her, praise and worship Her with a continuous dedication.

I am excited at the thought of closing my eyes in prayer and meditation,
...in an offering of my thanksgiving and appreciation
for Her love and salvation.
In the silence of my thoughts I can close my eyes
...in the stillness of my thoughts I can open my eyes and see the face of God.

I am mesmerized at Her artistry; taken aback at Her love
...I am left speechless
I am in awe.

I AM THAT I AM...and what she is,
is Nature's Beauty!

Shira Nicole Smith

Chapter 6

"Beyond the Physical, Why Should We Get Married": Adrianna and Kaylah

The naivety of youth

"Whenever I close my eyes, I can still see that naive fifteen-year-old girl, dating for the first time, completely submerged in the idea of what she thought love was", says Adrianna as she reflects on her childhood. She and my sister Shanice have been friends since the second grade. The two of them are inseparable. Sharing the same birthday, height, weight and similar facial features, with matching personalities, they have often been mistaken as twins.

"Swaying shyly on the swings in the park, getting my first kiss. I can remember the sweet letters, cute dates, and thoughtful gifts. Life was simple and it was fun, if only I knew then what I now know about marriage and relationships. My innocence had created an illusion that perhaps does not exist. But then again, I was seeing life through the eyes of an adolescent. As a 15-year-old girl I was shaped like a woman twice my age, but mentally and emotionally I was still very much like a child three years younger. So perhaps I shouldn't be so hard on myself and consider many of my experiences as honest mistakes caused by ignorance.

I was also ambitious with a clear cut plan for my life. Make a lot of money, get married, have kids, and live happily ever after watching the sunrise with my children and colourful evenings with my significant other while the golden glare of the sun sets across the azure ocean and sandy shores of Malibu, California. How hard could that be? I lived in this uninformed *illusion* for a long time until as the years went by, I realized life wasn't all wine and roses. Now two decades later, I am a divorced mother with two adopted kids, nothing had prepared me for this.

Happily, Ever After?

They say that *there is a thin line between love and hate*; my 'hersband' (how my partner prefers to be recognized as) and I were a living example of this adage. "Kaylah and Adrianna Collins, I now pronounce you hersband and wife", I can still hear our pastor's voice as her words echoed across the sanctuary. The cheers and excitement was euphoric. It was an amorous wedding, glamorous just as I envisioned when I was a little girl. Wow, I was so in love.

I was twenty-six when I married the *woman of my dreams* my Princess Queen what I liked calling her, whom like Valentine's candy I thought would *be mine forever*. She was ambitious, vibrant, and full of life. But my whimsical idea of marriage was short lived. Six years later I felt like I was living a fable and there was a big bad wolf huffing and puffing and doing all that it could to destroy my household. Oftentimes during the marriage, I wanted the wolf to kill this extremely pretty yet masculine woman whom had become my partner. Until now, two years after my divorce, I still do not understand how Kaylah and I went from being *so in love* and having sex five or six times a week, to hating the very mention of each other's names. I can still feel the way she handled my body, how she made love to me so tenderly. I was sprung: heart, mind, body and soul; every part of me belonged to her.

We were the 'it' couple among our friends before we got married having dated for a little over three years. We were always in sync, finished each other's sentences, went on the most romantic dates, grand adventures together, international vacations, and made so many plans for our future. Whatever we did, we did it together. We had shared many great memories over those three years that it wasn't a surprise when she finally asked me to marry her, we were convinced our union was written in the stars.

Now when I think about it, as clearly as the Big Dipper can be seen in the night time sky, I wish those stars would have formed the words "DON'T DO IT" across the heavens when we were planning our wedding. It would have spared us a lot of anguish. But it doesn't work that way now does it? I can remember the last year of our marriage like it all happened a few minutes ago. The woman that was once the most handsome and divine human being in my life had become a source of ugliness and dissatisfaction. I couldn't stand her for a second, and she didn't even want to be in the same room as me. When I compare this to how we started, I find myself deep in my thoughts with several blank spaces that I can't fill. Inside my mind it's like I'm in a maze with no exit.

The New Normal

Being divorced is not easy. Yes, you feel the freedom of not being in an emotionally draining situation anymore, but you need to be well-grounded in order to fully be comfortable with your new normal, and that takes a lot of dedication and discipline. It's particularly hard for me because I was raised in a family with Christian beliefs and therefore the pressure to live a traditional married life was overwhelming. Even more difficult was being in a same-sex relationship that my father, who's a well-known Pentecostal minister in our city, often publically denounced.

There are hundreds of religions in the world and each offer guidelines on a specific code of conduct that couples should adhere to in order to be on the *righteous path*. However, since I was raised as a Christian, I only know what Jesus Christ taught and each time I think about it, sometimes I'm overcome by feelings of guilt, failure, and betrayal of my faith. And because my sexuality contradicted this ideology I grew up tormented in a state of emotional and mental conflict. But all of this anguish vanished whenever Kaylah and I were together.

My parents have been married for over for forty-three years and they had hoped that I would follow in their footsteps. They are both devote Christians and their devotion to their faith and each other always served as motivation for my siblings and me, we all wanted the type of loving and respectable marriage that they have. After my divorce, my mom and dad had a lot to say, and their words were oftentimes very harsh. They were not happy with my decision. In their eyes I had sinned. But it takes a lot of courage to live openly as a lesbian woman raised under such a strict religious philosophy, and to get a divorce was a double whamming. Some couples, no matter how miserable they are refuse to divorce. But rather straight or gay I can't imagine living out the rest of my life in an unhappy marriage.

On a certain weekend, I decided to take my kids to my parent's house for a few days, and when we went to church that Sunday, the pastor was preaching about marriages. Until today, I'm still convinced my mother set it up. To be completely honest, the pastor said things that caused me to reflect upon my marriage, and for a while, what he said had me rethinking my divorce. And like times past his sermon put me in a state of turmoil that lasted for days. Concerned for my welfare and me not answering her calls, responding to her emails, or replying to her text messages for almost two days my best friend Shanice came to my house and found me in a disoriented state. She held me in her arms for hours as we both cried from the emotional pain I was suffering. Scouring the internet for a counsellor who could help me I discovered a 2-day singles and divorced women's retreat being hosted in two weeks and only a short distance from my home. Shanice agrees to attend the retreat with me. Although she has never been married she has endured the heart wrenching experience of a divorce when she and her ex-fiancé broke up after a five-year relationship.

Although the event seemed geared towards same-sex couples it was open to everyone. Here are some of the things I learned at this retreat:

The Spiritual Marriage Connection

According to the Bible verse Ephesians 5:25, husbands are instructed to love their wives as Christ loved the church while wives are advised to submit to their husbands. In my marriage, I was the spiritual one. My hersband was not a non-believer of Jesus Christ, but she wasn't committed to following the Christian philosophy either; so I guess my marriage was doomed from the very beginning. I had tried to make her understand how important religion was to me and how a little effort from her would be nice, but she never took me seriously. Never were it my intentions to convert her into my religion, but it was my desire for her to be more accommodating to my faith like I was with her free nature.

Some marriages have lasted a lifetime between partners who have completely different religious beliefs. I read somewhere that marriages between couples with different spiritual ideologies last when the partners are willing to learn from each other. Seek to understand my faith as I give attention to understanding your faith, then we can share what we learn without criticism or ridicule. We do not have to think the same, but respecting one another's religious perspective is a beautiful thing.

The Intimacy

One of the relationship therapist at the event shared a study highlighting that married people are much happier and are likely to live much longer than those who choose to live by themselves. Even more fascinating was that this conclusion was based upon the success of every type of marriage no matter their sexual orientation. She said "married couples share a spiritual intimacy that brings them closer and helps them achieve their purpose. Upon marriage, two individuals are joined together as one spirit (one universal energy), like nylon rope, created for superior strength and remarkable stretching capabilities and able to pull the heaviest loads while bearing the weight of the world. Two, is always better than one. This union was created by God to help build each other up, giving you a sense of importance which in turn boosts your confidence, helping you to grow into your best self."

Does this, therefore, mean now that I'm divorced I'm missing out on certain important elements that are important for personal growth. I have always trusted that belief in God was personal. That you can decide the kind of relationship you want to have with your God without copying anyone. Even now there are days when

I find myself questioning God and his plans for my life and intimate relationships, and many times I completely lose faith in experiencing the perfect relationship.

According to this study, partners help one another to keep believing in themselves. Spouses strengthen one another when the other becomes spiritually weak and stand with them until they are strong again and their spiritual intimacy is restored. Does this mean I can't do this for myself? I can go to a pastor for help, family members, and friends. However, this study further explains that the bond between married couples is different from the connection between friends, and that is why spiritual support in marriage is critical.

I honestly think that as long as I have my faith in check, whatever that means to me, I'm good. I don't need a marriage to get there. I could have never gotten there with my ex-hersband anyway because she believes religion is "brainwashing Idealism". Where were all these signs when we were dating? Love is a funny thing. Or perhaps I was blinded by lust.

The Identity

During the open discussion and questions and answers portion of the event Shanice shared a story of an occasion when she and her male ex-fiancé were invited to a party by some friends and somehow the group began talking about various sexual preferences that were once considered taboo but are now more acceptable in today's society; gay, bisexual, transgender, pansexual and everyone was contributing to the discussion giving insightful information. She said *"we were sharing, not judging and even those that did not agree with some of these categories, they were mature about it, giving their opinions without forcing it down anybody's throat. Then my ex comes up, speaking over everybody else and says, "gay people are lesser humans." At that moment, I was even ashamed of being linked to him, but hey, we were engaged to be married, if you see him, you see me. I hated being his fiancée at that moment, my identity that was linked to him began feeling like a burden."*

The therapist answered by sharing with us that "identity is a person's individuality, character, personality. We each have our own "identity", but so does your marriage. What is the personality of your marriage? How would people describe the character of your relationship? Marital identity is something a spiritually connected couple deal with every day. This is because your spouse is another physical and spiritual expression of you, whatever they are about is also a reflection upon you." Shanice went on to say that *"because my ex-fiancé and I had become so different, when I looked into his eyes I no longer saw the woman that I wanted to become. We lost the ability to inspire each other and drifted apart. I can now grasp the importance of being aware of your spiritual connection with your spouse because couples can build upon one another. What I can't do he can and vice versa. I'm 5'3" and my ex is 6'2", he could reach areas that I couldn't. But I was able to see things that he overlooked. Not only was this a benefit physically, but spiritually as well. Knowing this now I realize that this was one way that we showed genuine love to one another. However, anything contrary made me feel that the love was lost and the relationship had reached its conclusion."*

I interjected and shared that in my opinion, thinking back to my marriage with Kaylah, I realize that couples with similar religious beliefs in a Higher Deity have a reference or guidelines set out for them on how to conduct themselves towards each other so as not to embarrass their partners.

Now that I'm divorced, I can only depend on myself to keep me in check. Who's to say I won't let myself off the hook when I don't deserve it. My character will be according to what sits right with me and my feelings are not always right. I do not have someone I really trust in my everyday life to get their opinion. My growth will be my responsibility and if we're being honest, we all need help, even with ourselves. So I'm actually missing out on something important.

Sense of Security

Ironically, one of the certified marriage counsellors facilitating the event is a widower in her mid-forties who was married for eighteen years shared that *"one of the benefits of marriage is that life feels much easier during times when things get too much for you to handle alone, and you have that special person who makes everything feel less complicated. This is the same case with spirituality. In Christianity, the bible teaches us about an omnipotent Being who created the universe and everything in it. Through this Being you can do whatever you want and fulfil all of your heart's desires. This is why people pray when they need to be delivered from certain issues such as illness or issues that impact your relationship. Knowing that there is a God we can always turn to when things become too much for us is very reassuring and makes it easier to go about our normal life routines."* I struggled with believing that I could always turn to God for reassurance because of my sexuality and the dogmatic sermons preached condemning homosexuality from the leaders of the church. But Kaylah didn't care about what was being preached and her comforting words gave me confidence that I could always depend on her.

The therapist also shared that this sense of security is specifically reserved for marriages. The spiritual connection keeps the couple ever ready to come to each other's rescue no matter what the problem may be. This is often because your partner's problems become your own the moment you decide to become one in matrimony. Knowing that your partner will always look out for you can get you through many difficulties. It will motivate you to keep going and when both of you have your faith in the same supernatural power, it makes your confidence in whatever you're doing much stronger like nothing can stop you because you feel protected and secure.

Now being divorced I feel that I can only fully depend on myself. I do believe in God, don't get me wrong, but having someone to stand in full conviction with is what I do not have. The connection of having someone always there looking out for you without asking for anything in return is priceless and reassuring. Being without an intimate relationship is not always fun, no matter how necessary it may seem.

A Strong Friendship

Later that evening my confidant Shanice and I, along with two other ladies were discussing how important it is to be friends with your mate. Shanice made an excellent point when she shared that for a friendship to be considered strong, it means that even negative factors have been considered and they all cancel out. It is however not easy to forge such a friendship; it may take some work and patience.

All of the spiritual benefits we have discussed fully contribute to this. A friendship cannot stand the test of time without divine interference. A bond based on a sacred foundation is bound to last because both parties believe that the bedrock of their friendship is solid and that an infrastructure built upon this relationship will stand firm for decades to come.

Before people get married they are friends first (or at least should be), and then over time this friendship develops into a romantic connection. As teenagers Kaylah and I were the best of friends and ignored any intimate feelings and sexual urges out of fear of displeasing our families. For two people to elevate beyond a friendship, it means that they have completely put their trust and faith in the other person and are willing to accept all that comes with the relationship.

For those that are already married, they hope and pray that their partner appreciates all the effort they contribute to the marriage. For some people this may require belief in a Higher Power to influence their partners to be more openly to them. They slowly start seeing themselves in each other, growing together, and building a family and their spiritual connection keeps on getting stronger. They become inseparable best friends.

This philosophy was a difficult pill to swallow. I have missed having such an unconditional friend in my life. Kaylah and I fought a lot, but occasionally we rekindled the energy of being best friends like we had been years prior. We would laugh about stuff, help each other, and take care of one another. I admit that I have missed that feeling. That kind of connection we shared. But I'm single now, starting another connection like that from scratch feels overwhelming.

Spiritual View of Marriage

In Christianity, we are told that Christ loved the church so much that he died for it. My father preached this sermon many times. I can hear him saying to me specifically "Adrianna, Jesus was the son of God and his death signified that God still wants us to be part of his spiritual family." My reply is that one's sexuality should have no barring when it comes to receiving the spiritual benefits of marriage. My sexuality and spirituality aren't synonymous.

We are also told that in the last days, "Christ will marry the church, and they shall be one in glory. This means that Jesus will come back to take the righteous into eternal salvation. This signifies a strong spiritual bond that cannot be broken, Adrianna"; my dad would say.

However, what he did not say was that in many scenarios this bond is developed slowly. In my opinion, people should be given the choice to choose if they want to accept this religious ideology as their reality or not.

My dad feels that all couples should take the time to reconnect to this "strong spiritual bond that cannot be broken". I feel that rather than force your beliefs upon your spouse, you each should at least consider exploring this "spiritual awakening" together even if you don't agree, in hopes of reaping the benefits of understanding one another and how it feels to value your differences within your holy matrimony.

Here are a few pointers:

- **Don't rush**; one partner may be perceived as more devotional than the other. He or she shouldn't pressure the other person to measure up. They should let them get there on their own, allow them to decide what they want to believe in and how they want to practice it.

- **Discover yourself**; it is impossible to form any sort of connection if you do not know who you are first and what you desire. You need to give yourself time to discover your "spiritual identity" and learn how to be comfortable in it.

- **Don't be too ambitious**; once you taste the satisfaction and reassurance that comes with spiritual awakening, you may be tempted to go all-in immediately. However, it is important to never forget that your marriage is your first ministry. You may feel like it's important to spend as much time in your devotion but during that time your spouse may be feeling neglected. Remember this, there is no greater commitment to God than the time you dedicate to experiencing the love of God through your spouse. No greater delight is there than the joy that comes from God through your significant other.

So How is my Spiritual Awakening as a Divorced Woman?

First of all, I completely stand with my decision to get a divorce. I was in a situation that needed to end and in another lifetime, I would still do the same thing.

I have come to realize that to be spiritually receptive, you need to be ready to free yourself from anything that is holding you back. Open your heart and mind and be ready to receive from God.

However, I've also learned that I made several mistakes when I decided to marry my ex-hersband.

To begin with, she had no spiritual grounding which meant she had no boundaries, no moral code, and neither was she in touch with her inner being. By marrying her, I had allowed her to pull me into her world of confusion and almost lost myself. There was nothing else for us to connect upon beyond the physical.

I can work on my spiritual growth, it may be hard working alone, but it is better than working with someone with zero interest in what's important to me.

What about Marriages?

There's a universal idea that since the beginning of time, through Adam and Eve, the institution of marriage was created. Some would say that marriage was initially all about procreation and building a family. However, over time, many opinions have been given that marriage has become more of a platform where people seek a much deeper connection.

With the right partner, this profound alliance can lead to metaphysical levels of intimacy beyond what you never thought were possible. But with the wrong person, you may be led into outer darkness, blindsided and confused, having forgotten the person whom you once were prior to the relationship.

A deep spiritual connection is very important for all couples; it keeps them strong. It brings them closer to one another and allows them to keep learning and discovering each other as the marriage ages. They just have to make sure that they always nurture this relationship.

Conclusion

When you get divorced, it does not mean that your spiritual bond with yourself is dead. Your partnership with your spouse may have been cut short, but your spiritual relation with yourself should and can remain strong when you remember to be kind and to love thyself first.

If you are a Christian like me, do not let the pressure overwhelm you. Seeking peace for yourself is not a crime. It may be scary when you consider the religious conversations that condemn divorce and a non-traditional sexual orientation, but always remember you owe it to yourself to be happy. You cannot forge a strong physical connection if an outdated spiritual theory is causing you distress.

At this point in my life, I choose to flow with what makes my heart smile. The thought of all the spiritual benefits I'm missing out on being single is saddening but then considering I wasn't getting them in my previous marriage makes this pill much easier to swallow.

There were a lot of women at the retreat that have been bruised and battered by a bad relationship, especially this young lady named Cora. She seemed so sad and heartbroken; her low energy was crippling, and she wore the scars of being emotionally beaten across her face. After watching her that weekend, I do not know if I'll ever get married again or if I'm ready to confront that idea yet. All I care about right now is how far I can go alone spiritually and so far so good.

CHAPTER 7:
It Wasn't Satan, God Ruined My Marriage
Dylan and Cora

July 10, 2005.

"We really need to get out of here now or we're going to be late for church. There's going to be a special guest speaker today"; said Dylan.

"I don't want to go; let's stay at home this evening. We are always at church", Cora exclaims.

"But the Bible says that we are supposed to keep the Sabbath Day holy and go to church. We're going to church", speaking to her as if she was a child.

"I'm your husband and the head of this house; you're supposed to obey me."

She storms off into the bathroom to apply her makeup and continues getting dressed for church.

"I can't stand him and I hate this stupid church", Cora thinks to herself; anger and rage vibrating through her entire body. *"All that Pastor talks about are rules and how every action done that is not aligned with the Bible will cause people to go to Hell. Is there anything that we can do that's fun that doesn't attribute to going to purgatory?"*

"We can't do this; we can't do that; blah blah blah. All I want to do is spend some time with my husband and every so often go out with my friends. What's so bad about that?", she inquires of herself.

"LET'S GO!" He yells to her from the living room. She grabs her purse and rushes out the house and into the car.

"You are so fucking slow! Why does it take you so goddamn long getting ready? This makes no sense. It's like you're retarded or something. Are you fucking retarded?", he screams at her with malice and disgust in his voice. **"You're so stupid!** *And now we're going to be late. You know how much that I hate being late."*

"I'm sorry", she whispers softly in an attempt not to anger him any further.

"Yeah you are sorry", he replied condescendingly.

A tear flows down her right eye and drags with it the makeup that she spent forty-five minutes applying.

Sitting quietly in the passenger seat she begins to thinks *"Why does God hate me so much? What did I do to deserve being treated this way? I thought marrying Deacon Dylan Andrews would be different than marrying a man who works in another profession.* Multiple voices in her head replied *"he was so nice when we met that night at his uncle's church a year ago. But let's be honest we weren't physically attracted to him anyway; he's not cute and has no sex appeal at all, and is horrible in bed.* Cora replies, *but he's a minister; he's supposed to be a man who has the heart of God. He's supposed to be a man who knows how to treat a woman, be kind to her, and love and honor her. At least that's the promise that he made to me when he begged me to marry him."*

They arrive into the church parking lot, found a spot about 30 yards from the main entrance, and rushed inside to be seated in the upper balcony as the choir began to sing the first of many praise and worship songs.

"Welcome Deacon Andrews; Sister Andrews", said the Usher as they entered Faith Tabernacle Baptist Church of Compton.

"Thank You Sister", he replied with the traditional sanctified response that is so popular amongst many churchgoers.

"He's such a fake", Cora says to herself. Yet she smiles and replies with the same response. *"God bless you sister"*, as she nods while walking to their seats inside of this 5000 seat sanctuary.

An hour and half into the church service the guest speaker is announced and begins his sermon.

"Praise the Lord saints. I said PRAISE THE LORD Saints", the minister yells into the microphone. The church roars and celebrates Jesus for another 10 minutes.

"I wish he would get this sermon over with so we can go home in time for me to watch an episode of Real Housewives of Atlanta", Cora jokingly whispers to the lady sitting next to her.

The guest pastor continues with his sermon.

"I was praying last night asking God for a message to share with you today; a Word from the Lord that is necessary and will greatly impact your life.

And the Word came to me as clearly as the day is long. ***BEASTIALITY****! This is a message from God specifically for married couples, because some of you are sinning against*

God and don't even know it. Again, Cora whispers in her neighbor's ear *"Does he mean Beastiality? As in sex with animals?* Looking around they realized that everyone seemed equally confused.

"You all are engaging in lascivious behaviors while having sex, yet all the while not realizing that God is displeased with your actions."

Cora was scrolling through her phone uninterested in the Pastor until he mentioned that God is displeased with she and Dylan's sex life. This peaked her interest more because she thought that she was the only one who was displeased with their sex life. His *shortcomings*, as she refers to Dylan's sexual abilities has caused her significant dissatisfaction. The only sexual enjoyment she derives from each encounter is when it's over and she can pleasure herself without his *'assistance'.*

"Performing oral sex on each other and intercourse in the doggy style position is an abomination to God. Your marriage is failing because of your sexual perversions. You need to stop this NOW!" he screamed into the microphone.

*"**REPENT!** And turn from your wicked ways; and give your marriage back to God. No sexual pleasures can*

compete with the love of God. Don't risk eternity in Hell for a few minutes of oral copulation."

Cora sat completely erect on the edge of her seat, mouth fully ajar, in total disbelief of what she was hearing, and fearing the worst of what was to come from today's message *"from God"*. She looked over at Dylan to see if he was in agreement with the Pastor, and as always he did so agree.

"Amen Pastor! You're preaching well", he shouted out loud.

In that moment her eyes began to water because she knew that her chances of having an orgasm while they were intimate had just been banished from their bedroom and *cast into the depths of Hades.* Dylan would no longer comply with performing cunnilingus, and what she liked about doggy style was not having to look at Dylan during relations. For her, the demise of their marriage was inevitable.

Church service ended with the usual handshakes and hugs, small talk, and fake promises to stay in touch and pray for one another. But Cora and Dylan's car ride home was completely different. Again she quietly sat in the passenger seat with no other voices in her head to contemplate the "word of God" expounded by the visiting pastor, and this time also in a state of shock.

"Dylan, Beastiality is sex with animals, do you agree with what Pastor said that having sex in the doggy-style position and oral sex in marriage is an abomination and the same as Beastiality? How can our sexual relations as human beings be the same thing? Do you believe that these acts are sins?"

"Damn right it's a sin", he said with certainty.

"So what does this mean for us? Are we going to stop engaging in these acts when we're having sex", she asked with an expression of grievance in her voice?

"You damn right we are going to stop doing that shit. Hell no, I'm not going to allow you to force me into sin and displeasing God because you want me to go down on you. Fuck that shit!"

"Do you feel that cursing is a sin", she asked so that she can draw his attention to his quick use of foul language so soon after leaving holy grounds.

"Actually I do not feel that cursing is a sin because there's cursing in the Bible. But there is nothing in the Bible that says anything about oral sex or doing it in the doggie style position. That's how animals have sex, and we're not animals. And like I said before, I'm not going to hell for doing that crap."

The argument continued throughout that day and the upcoming weeks about what are acceptable sexual acts between the two of them. And the miserable, unhappiness, and lonely nights together continued.

Six weeks later.

"We need to go to marriage counseling like right now. This isn't working for me anymore", Dylan said as they were watching the latest religious program on the *700 Club*.

"I am unhappy", he said.

"YOU ARE UNHAPPY?? she said in a loud but confusing voice. *NIGGA, I KNOW MOTHERFUCKING WELL YO ASS AIN'T SAYING NO SHIT LIKE THIS TO ME!*

I have been unhappy with your ugly ass since day one. The only reason why I'm still married to you is because everyone keeps telling me it's a sin to divorce, and how I need to be patient. I'm tired of people telling me that this is normal; every couple goes through this. MAN FUCK THAT! And nigga fuck you to!"

She laid back on the couch seething in indignation.

"You can curse me out all you want. Get it out now before we meet with the pastor tomorrow evening", said Dylan.

"You scheduled marriage counseling with the pastor... without telling me first? Are you crazy? I don't want to talk to him!" The argument ensued long into the night until Cora finally conceded to counseling with their pastor.

The next evening, they attended their 7:30pm one-hour marriage counseling session with Pastor Savoy.

"Welcome Deacon, and Sister."

The Pastor extends his arms for a hug from the two of them. But Cora is certainly not in the mood for fake hugs and the usual *meet and greet*, and makes it apparent that she doesn't want to be there.

"Sister Cora, I sense that something is bothering you. Tell me what's on your mind?"

"Talk to Dylan, Pastor, because it was his idea to schedule this counseling session."

"Dylan tells me that there's trouble at home and that he feels that you all may be on the verge of a separation. Is that right Sister Cora?"

"It's whatever he says Pastor Savoy. It's ALWAYS whatever HE says."

"But I'm the man of the house; it's supposed to be whatever I say"; sounding indignant Dylan replied.

"Hold on son; let me talk to Cora for a moment. You just sit there and listen; I'll tell you when to chime in. Cora, is it true what Dylan says about your unhappiness with your current sex life?"

"I've always been unhappy with our 'current sex life', Pastor. But the message that was preached a few weeks ago about how certain sexual acts are an abomination to God is ridiculous, and for me that was the straw that broke the camel's back."

"Tell me why you feel that what was taught was ridiculous. Do you not believe in the Bible? Don't you believe in God? Don't you want to go to heaven?"

"Pastor Savoy, I am convinced that religion ruins marriages."

Both the pastor and Dylan sat back in their chairs staring at Cora because of the *blasphemy* that has just come out of her mouth.

"Religion is like politics; everyone has an opinion and only feels that their way of thinking and belief is the only right way to think or believe.

But the reality is that NO ONE knows what's best for our marriage better than the two people in the marriage. How would you feel if Dylan or myself told you how to make love to your wife? You and First Lady Savoy have been married for 38 years. So how could MY husband tell YOU how to please YOUR wife? He's not the man screwing your wife. So how would he know what is sexually pleasing to YOUR wife?"

"Now wait a goddamn minute young Lady, " the pastor exclaims. *How dare you talk to me in that manner? You are being disrespectful and I demand your respect, Cora!"*

"How am I being disrespectful Pastor? Exasperated, Cora replied, *you allowed another minister to stand in YOUR pulpit and told MY husband how he should make love to me. And now you sit there in agreement with that foolishness. Isn't that what we're talking about? YOU don't know my body; you and I have never had sex; and other than our greetings during church service we at no time have had a conversation until today. So how is it possible for you to know what is gratifying to me?*

It is no more possible for you to know me than it is for my husband to know how to sexually please your wife. I would NEVER ask your wife how to satisfy my man.

Now you may offer some suggestions! But the truth is that the ONLY person who knows what is pleasurable to themselves is THAT PERSON.

Standing, and then walking towards the door to leave, she turns and says *"Dylan doesn't need to be discussing with you what pleases me. HE SHOULD BE TALKING TO ME! He is supposed to love me in the same way that Christ loves the church; in that he is willing to make sacrifices for me. What pleases me is pleasing to God because it means that we are "living happily ever after". And if the only way that I can have an orgasm is when he performs cunnilingus then goddamn it that's the fucking sacrifice he needs to make!"* she said with anger and force as she stormed out of the room.

The next day Cora scheduled an appointment to meet with a divorce attorney, and shortly thereafter Dylan was served with Dissolution of Marriage papers. After almost a two-year battle in divorce court the marriage was dissolved. Taking actions with the advice she received during the relationship retreat a few years ago, and outlining specifically what she wanted to enjoy in a relationship and experience with a mate; soon after Cora met, fell in love and married her soul mate, and currently living her best (sex) life possible. As she would say in a nonchalant way, *"all things work together for your good. There's a calling upon my life to be happy, and that's exactly how I intend to live."*

CHAPTER 8

Ask for What You Want in a Mate

"Excuse me sir, do you have a dollar that you can spare?"

Enraptured by my own thoughts as I hurriedly along to meet up with Anthony, my friend and roommate from college, when my concentration was interrupted by a homeless man beseeching me for alms. He held a sign that read "donations please", and before he could verbalize his request I had already decided that I wasn't going to admonish his appeal. But for some reason as he spoke to me I was compelled to listen to him.

"Any amount would be helpful so that I can get something to eat."

I wasn't convinced by his sales spiel because I was certain that he was not going to use the money to get anything to eat. However, that didn't concern me anyway.

"One dollar? In this day and age, what are you going to eat with one dollar?"

"Well if you can spare more than a dollar that would be even more appreciated", he said to me.

"Would you be happy if I give you two dollars?", I asked.

"For sure. Thank you so much!"

"Sir, it's 2019! We're in southern California, are you going to buy something to eat with only two dollars? A McDonald's McMuffin meal cost almost $10."

"Well, I'm hoping that other people would be as kind to help me out with any spare change until I have enough to buy myself a McDonald's McMuffin meal."

"This guy is such a terrible salesman", I think to myself while pulling out the $500 I had in my pocket. I slowly counted it out in front of him so that he could see that I had far more money to spare than the amount that he asked for. His eyes widened with surprise and he became excited at the thought that perhaps I would give him more than what he had asked.

"Here you go, Sir. I hope this helps."

With a look of shock upon his face and agitation in his voice he replied "TWO DOLLARS! That's all you're going to give me?"

"That's all that you asked for. You should be grateful. God answered your prayer. If you wanted more you should have asked for more. I asked you twice what you are going to buy with $1 or $2, and you never asked for more than two dollars. You were not honest with yourself and too afraid to specify to me the amount you truly wanted in your request; therefore, I gave to you exactly what you asked for.

Haven't you learned in all your years that you will never get out of life what you don't ask for!"

And as I walked away I was reminded of a powerful lesson that I learned from Anthony *"you will never attract TO you what you do not believe is possible FOR you."*

Often, many single individuals will only ask for the type of relationship that they feel they deserve versus what they are worthy of receiving. Some may wish for more but over time tend to pick away at their wish list when the perfect mate has not arrived as quickly as desired.

But the truth is that you are worthy of (and deserve) so much more.

You will never manifest that fantasy relationship until you are specific in what you want to enjoy in your relationship and experience with your mate.

So how do you create a relationship or marriage that matches what you think you are worthy of, by *asking for it*? Even if you don't believe that you will receive it, keep asking until you do believe it. And then once you believe it, live on that vibration as if you have already received it. Become the spouse that you desire to be for your significant other by acting as if you are already married to the perfect mate.

Take some time and draw it out on paper. Take your fantasy and the images of what you feel a good intimate connection looks like for you and put it in writing. Be clear-cut. Definitive. And if you don't already have an image in your mind find other couples that mirror what your heart tells you would be good for you. Ask for the love and intimacy that your soul wants to connect with; not for what your brain tells you that you can get.

Vanish all negative thoughts, talks, and ideas about marriage from your mindset. Some women will spend all night praying for their ideal mate, and then spend all day talking themselves out of it. Guard your tongue with diligence. It is imperative that you do not say anything that is contrary to what you desire to encounter. If you want a good, loving, romantic, wealthy, smart husband, do not spend your days making statements like "men ain't shit"; "all men are dogs"; "every man I meet is broke"; "all the good men are already taken", and other popular derogatory phrases about men.

And fellas, you can't be hanging out with your male friends dogging out women, calling them bitches and whores, and demeaning them for their past sexual encounters, or bad decisions that may have been made during their previous relationships. Discussing these things is counterproductive to your quest for finding a "good woman"; attracting your Queen; and building a legacy with the woman of your dreams.

"If you can't see it with your mind first, you'll never see it with your eyes." -Anthony Lamar Smith, LIFEstyle Improvement Coach

You attract *to* you what is *within* you. To attract the perfect mate, you must *become* the perfect mate. Take some time and analyze who you are as a person. Would you date yourself? Are you honest with or do you lie to yourself? Ladies, is your fantasy guy healthy, slim, and fit, but you're out of shape and unhappy with your body type, would this fantasy guy find you attractive? Men, is the lady in your imagination an accomplished woman whose college educated with an amazing career, but you are an unemployed high school dropout?

A few people may say that this sounds superficial, but sometimes being *"politically correct"* will have you thinking *incorrectly* and keep you from experiencing the married life of your dreams.

Always remember, you deserve to live...

"Happily, Ever After"

ROSE!

Today

I looked into the eyes of a flower

...and I saw You.

I heard the enchanting sounds of your voice

...as your melody danced upon the aura vibrating from its fragrance.

I could feel the pleasure of your touch

...as the spirit of LOVE flowed through its veins to bring beauty into my LIFE.

I admired its shape

...and adored the tightness of your silky skin enwrapped around each petal.

I slowly brought the flower closer to me and softly slide it across my lips

...so that I could taste the essence of your kiss.

Today

I looked into the *eyes of a Rose* and I saw

...YOU!

The Married LIFE / *Anthony Lamar Smith*

Chapter 9:
Happily, Ever After
Ant & Shira

"Successful marriages are visualized and created in the mind first then experienced in the body. And so is a bad marriage. Nothing happens by accident. Every experience today is a result of thoughts and decisions visualized and internalized throughout your past. To get from point A to point B there has to be a roadmap that starts from your current destination and ends at your desired destination".

Once a week, at his home office, my friend Anthony shares some powerful precepts and proven steps to help us live our best life possible. This week he's discussing marriage and how he and his wife Shira attracted each other and enjoy such a wonderful marriage. Entering their home and walking slowly into the large family room, quietly I take a seat at the back of the room as not to disturb the group that has gathered;

Anthony has already started the conversation about creating and living your best marriage imaginable.

"Last week we discussed the bad reputation that marriage has; this ridiculous notion that *marriage is hard work.* Let us conclude that a failed marriage is 'point B' and the idea that marriage is hard is 'point A'; starting a relationship with this philosophy embedded in your psyche will lead to the demise of your marriage. If you accept that marriage is hard, for you it will always be arduous, complicated, and sometimes cruel.

For instance, a lot of employees hate or dislike their jobs very much. Which is why the vast majority of heart attacks happening on Monday mornings are because people dread going to work. A *"marriage is hard work mindset"* will eventually kill you. If not physically killing you, it'll definitely deprive you of your joy, your happiness, and peace of mind; and destroy all chances of living and enjoying a successful marriage *until death do us part.*

Charles Haanel, author of the bestselling book "The Master Key System" wrote "all mistakes are but the mistakes of ignorance. Knowledge gaining and consequent use of this *power* is what determines growth and evolution."

To experience a good marriage, each of you in the relationship most first accept that a good marriage is a reality, and secondly obtaining the knowledge of how to create a satisfying marriage is what's necessary to experience and enjoy living happily, ever after.

Recently, my friend Sean asked *is it really possible for a couple to actually create a marriage that can be enjoyed by both people from start to finish.* The reality is that no one goes through a lifetime without ever encountering difficulties and challenges that affect you emotionally. Of course Shira and I have had issues in our marriage that may have led other couples to divorce. The difference is that we have realized that there is a difference between issues within our marriage versus issues that affect our marriage. Later I will share with you a list of areas in your relationship that every couple should pay attention to; you're welcome to add to this list based upon what's important to your marriage.

I am married to my wife...not our children. Therefore, we won't allow our parenting differences to destroy our relationship. We married each other...and not our in-laws. Therefore, there is nothing that our parents or siblings can say or do that we will allow to destroy the love that we enjoy. Early on, I came into the relationship with some major financial issues and credit challenges, but my wife's money management skills and our ability to be creative with even the smallest amount of money left over after our bills were paid afforded us the chance to create some of our most memorable "date nights".

Shira and I met on Facebook before it became the most popular social media platform. Browsing through her photos I was immediately attracted to her physically, but when we finally met in person I became more captivated by her energy, spirit and fun personality. And for her, feelings about me was mutual.

Because we both endured the misery of a failed marriage and divorce we agreed that marriage wasn't an option for us. Our connection was strong and we had fallen deeply in love and was happy with the way things were between us. But as our relationship progressed and our affection grew more intense, driven by divine inspiration we chose to tie the knot.

Couples living in a successful marriage make it their business to hold the ideals of a loving, fun, exciting, vibrant, healthy, energetic, prosperous marriage as a desire that they wish to someday realize. Once they have conceived of what this quintessential marriage looks like for them, they then take action to create it and live in its fullness every day.

To manifest and experience a good marriage it must be treated in the same manner a CEO and board members operate a successful business. Your marriage must have a purpose and goals that are clearly defined. And each area of the relationship should be run similarly to sections of a department store are operated.

While at the mall one day I walked into a popular department store and noticed a woman being irate with one of the sales representatives in the shoe department. Apparently the customer wanted assistance in the purse section. The sales rep politely told the customer that she doesn't work in that department but would page over the intercom someone to assist her. The customer went on to say that she had been waiting at the checkout for over five minutes for someone to help her, and began questioning why the sales rep in the shoe department couldn't help her. The shoe department was packed with other patrons who also needed attention, consumers who were actually buying shoes. Politely, the sales representative stated that she couldn't leave her department to service her with finding the particular purse that she wanted to purchase. The indignant woman became belligerent and caused an unnecessary scene. Finally, a store manager came along to defuse the situation and assist the customer with purchasing her purse and allowing the sales rep to continue servicing the other customers in the shoe department.

After witnessing this argument and as I walked around I came upon a sign that read that the department store was founded in the mid-1800s. A company that has been in business for over 160 years must have a proven track record for its success. I believe that one area of its success is that each store is divided into multiple sections and departments. Each section is a small business within the larger organization which is led by a Manager who hires, trains, and helps the employees service the customers that visit that particular division. Employees of the shoe department do not service customers in the purse section. Each employee is assigned to a "storefront" and become experts who specialize in the products in that area of the company. This is a benefit to the overall success of the business.

When developing and realizing a fruitful marriage that endures, it has to be managed like a department store. Each area of your marriage should be established and must have annual, semi-annual, and monthly goals. And the objectives for your marriage must be revisited often to discover where the relationship is thriving and were it needs improving. Here is a list of the departments that Shira and I pay close attention to:

1. Communication.

2. Sex.

3. Health and wellness.

4. Career and Goals.

5. Financial and money management.

6. Children and discipline.

8. Travel department.

9. In-laws.

Your marriage is a "spiritual body". And like the physical body if you cut your finger, although the pain is not felt throughout the whole body, the entire anatomy suffers because that one finger is hurting. No thought is given to other areas of the body; all attention is given to the part that is in pain. You don't think about your feet when your stomach hurts. However, you do everything that you can to stop the ache so that the entire body will feel whole again.

Shira and I we have listed these departments in order of importance for our marriage, you may decide to outline them differently. Either way be sure to give as much consideration to these areas to ensure your marriage endures the test of time.

Communication Department

One characteristic of our relationship that caused me to fall in love with Shira was our ability to have the best conversations. Even unto to this day we still talk and laugh for hours at a time. What a refreshing feeling it is to have a spouse whom I can talk to like she's my best friend. Because she is my best friend. Take a moment to reflect on how wonderful it feels when you are talking to your friends. What makes our conversations so intimate is how well we talk to each other. In short, communication is intimacy. Couples feel a deep affection to their partner when each person listens without interruptions and judgement, and honors and respects what the other person is trying to convey. To feel connected does not mean that there's always an agreement regarding a topic or issue. Intimacy is felt when both parties feels acknowledged and heard when you are in disagreement.

Remember, although the two of you are married and have become "one" spiritually; you are still two complete individuals with your own opinions, values, behaviors. Misunderstandings and ineffective communication is exhausting and will negatively impact other areas of your life. Arguments, name calling, or not giving your spouse the undivided attention they deserve can be crippling to your relationship.

Sex Department

For us this area is extremely important because we thoroughly enjoy the physical act of making love to each other. It's fun. And it's healthy. Many studies have proven that there are a lot of physical, mental, spiritual and emotional benefits to a good active sex life. Physical attraction is what draws a couple together. No man can see a woman's personality, character, if she's loyal and faithful, or has a great sense of humor when he first looks at her. His immediate attraction is to her physical beauty. And likewise for women. Notice how when asked what a woman wants in a mate many women often start by stating something physical about him. And for those who don't put as much importance on a man's physical attributes she still has in mind what her "fantasy guy" looks like. So being physically attracted to your mate adds great value to your sex life. Which is why health and wellness being critical to a successful relationship.

Health and Wellness

Let's face it, a marriage can't endure if you're dead. Nor is it beneficial to the overall health of the relationship when you are suffering from some type of illness or sickness. Having a chronic ailment such as diabetes, arthritis, mental or physical disabilities and other diseases can take a toll on even the best relationship.

The partner who's sick may not feel, or act/react as intimately the way they did before the illness. And the person who's not sick may not know how to deal with this new reality. The strain may push both people's understanding of *"in sickness and in health"* to its breaking point.

Studies reveal that relationships in which one spouse has a chronic illness are more likely to fail if the spouses are young or early on in the marriage. And spouses who are caregivers are six times more likely to be depressed than spouses who do not need to be caregivers.

Being sick can weigh heavy on every part of your relationship and can rob you of many years of wedded bliss. Yes, traditional vows state "in sickness and in health". But the reality is no one marries for "in sickness". Of course, I don't advocate divorcing your spouse if he/she is stricken with an illness. I'm simply stating that it is radically important that you do what's necessary to maintain a healthy vibrant body so you can live for many years and for your spouse to enjoy until your death comes by natural causes.

Medical problems do not just impact the relationship emotionally but can also destroy couples, financially. So if or when "in sickness" comes into your relationship and you begin to feel overwhelmed by this crisis affecting the overall health of your marriage, never feel ashamed to seek professional counseling for solutions that will help restore the vitality to your union.

Financial and Money Management Department

Money. It is often said that money can't buy happiness; as if to suggest that those whom struggle financially are "happy". No man is happy being unable to provide for his family; there is no honor in being broke. Be not deceived by anything contrary because it's a wonderful feeling to be financially successful. Being able to provide a comfortable lifestyle for yourself and family free of stress and worry raises a person's confidence and self-esteem.

The boyfriend who surprises his girlfriend with a Valentine's Day gift also *bought* her jubilant reaction when the flowers, candy, and a love note is received. The opposite is experienced when he doesn't have the money to surprise his lady with a gift.

A mom looking into the eyes of a cheerful child when she presents her youngster with their favorite birthday present. A husband beaming with pride while witnessing the joy on his wife's face when he gives her an anniversary gift. A wife feeling safe and secure and able to rest in her bed peacefully when all of the bills are paid is an exhilarating emotion that was *bought* with money.

Money is simple a medium of exchange, a tool that is used to barter with. Perhaps money can't buy joy, but it sure does give you the ability to purchase things and experiences for the people who add happiness to your life and to friends, family, and loved-ones whom you want to make happy for that moment in time.

Finances are one of the primary reasons couples seek guidance from a marriage counselor, as limited funds and past due bills can cause a lot of grief. A lack of money or even a gap in how much money each partner contributes can lead to power struggles or imbalances between the two of you. This can cause problems in the marriage that may be hard to repair; which is why it is vitally important to discuss how the finances should be handle.

Perhaps one of you manage money better than the other; give permission to your spouse to oversee this department. Shira is fiscally conservative and I am an emotional buyer. I like to buy what I want when I want it. Although we both are high income earners, I would be broke if I didn't listen and heed to my wife's advice most of the time. Much of our financial success is because of how well she governs our money. And she has also admitted that she wouldn't have enjoyed many of the extravagant memories we've created if she didn't submit to some of the high-cost things that I enjoy providing for our family. The bottom-line is that there has to be balance in this department.

Children and Discipline department

Constant quarrels. Relentless bickering is a red flag. Many couples in troubled relationships typically repeat the same arguments, especially when it's about the kids. There was a time in my life when I was convinced that having, providing for, and raising children ruined relationships. When two people can't see each other's point of view when it involves raising and disciplining their kids, arguments don't get resolved and resentment can grow. I strongly believe that each parent's intentions are pure even when mistakes are made while the children are minors.

The problem starts when both parents strongly believe that the way they were raised is the "right way" for upbringing a kid. When a couple refuses to see eye-to-eye, they may be in danger of divorce without professional help to solve these challenges. Hiring a parenting coach and learning various disciplinary tactics that each parent can respect and adhere to is healthy for the marriage and increases the odds of successfully raising your children.

Travel department

Couples who travel together have healthier, happier relationships compared to those who do not, according to a survey from the U.S. Travel Association. Couples in a romantic relationship report traveling together makes them significantly more likely to be satisfied in their relationships, communicate well with their partners, enjoy more romance, spend valuable time together loving on and appreciating each other, dream about and make plans for their future, and enjoy a better sex life. Although my wife and I enjoy an excellent sex life in the privacy of our home, but some of our more explosive and passionate experiences were created when we were enjoying our time together in some of the world's most romantic vacation destinations.

In-laws

When one spouse has a primary attachment to someone that is stronger than the devotion to their partner -- be it a close friend, a parent, or a child -- the marriage is in trouble. Financial issues and challenges with raising children are complicated enough, adding meddling in-laws into the mix is a recipe for disaster. It is essential that you and your spouse realize that you are married to each other and not to your in-laws. As a husband please understand that your wife is not in a marriage with your mom. As much as you may love your mom and have a close relationship with her, your mom does not come first before your wife. Your mother does not have the right to come into the home that you share with your wife and boss her around. Boundaries must be set. Your mother has her own life to live and manage; therefore, her opinions about how your wife manages the affairs of your home is none of your mother's business.

As a wife instill this in your psyche, your dad is not your man and no longer has any "authority" over you. As long as your husband is not causing you physical harm your father is not responsible for your well-being. You and your husband made a commitment to one another. An allegiance that includes creating and establishing a life together unencumbered by in-laws or any other individual's negative influences. Never bash or speak ill of your husband to your father, brothers, uncles, or other male relatives or friends. Doing so will minimize how your husband is perceived amongst these men. No greater disrespect will a man endure than when his wife is degrading him to other men.

And as a couple, never share with your spouse anything unfavorable that your family says about them, and don't allow your family to make derogatory statements about your significant other. This will only cause more problems for the two of you. Sound advice and opinions are completely different. Positive thoughts about marriage and constructive suggestions that will benefit your relationship and help it progress are welcome. Anything contrary must be dismissed immediately.

Contrary to a popularly distorted belief, marriage is fun. But when couples rush into a lifetime union without fully understanding the institution of marriage they face confrontations that can cause each partner to feel overwhelmed. Which is why when Shira and I decided to wed, we identified ***FIVE PRECEPTS*** that if applied consistently, will lead to your ideal marriage as long as you shall live.

Precept 1. **Identify your WHY**: draft a list of <u>FIVE compelling reasons why</u> marriage and being married to your spouse is important to you. The reasoning can't be "on the surface ideas". Go within. Take some time to meditate upon this topic until you have internally, psychologically, and emotionally identified why creating and living in a successful marriage with this person is an absolute MUST for you.

Precept 2. **Dream BIG**: create a visual of how you want your marriage to look and feel like. Search for couples that are living in the type of marriage that you would want to enjoy. And then emulate them; pattern yourselves after them. But make sure that your partner agrees with your vision and the couple you want to model for your relationship. What you desire for the marriage may be different from your spouse. It's okay to have differences. Learn from your dissimilarities and design a plan to include both of your desires into your marriage. And "dream bigger" by including into that vision what is uniquely the two of you. Although a lot of marriages may look alike by outer appearance; every married couple has something that is unique to their marriage. What is that "one thing" that makes your relationship extraordinary?

Precept 3. **Draft a Plan** for the marriage and analyze or revise the plan often until your marriage becomes exactly as you want it to be. Remember, your marriage is a lifetime commitment to each other. Treat it like a business that will be in existence throughout multiple generations. Therefore, over time your plan will need to be modified often. And it is okay if your first plan or the first 10 plans that have been drafted for the marriage doesn't work out. When this happens, revert back to *Precept 1* to be reminded of your compelling reasons **WHY** having a successful marriage with your spouse is an absolute MUST for you.

Precept 4: **Get Excited!** Be delighted, enthusiast, and passionate about your marriage. And instill this into your mind, that *there is a difference between motivation versus inspiration*. Motivation is temporary and based upon what is currently happening in your marriage at that time. But inspiration is that sensation that burns inside of you all the time.

After speaking with people who have gone through a divorce and reflecting upon my failed marriage, what is mentioned often is that the couples were no longer "happy" in their relationship. They had lost all motivation to stay in the marriage. Happy is short for happiness, and it is an emotional term to describe how you currently feel about a particular thing or scenario. But it is a fleeting emotion because things and scenarios change often.

However, inspiration comes from within. It's an energy that keeps you alive and well, and constantly moving in the direction that's best for you. And to be inspired to accomplish a particular goal is ignited by a strong emotional need or compelling reasons *why* it is an *absolute must,* and then doing what is necessary to manifest this particular desire. Which brings us to our next axiom.

Precept 5: **Take Action NOW**: In most instances, people who fulfill their dreams and goals do so by *failing* their way to success. Never in the history of massive success has anyone been able to achieve a goal upon his or her first course of action.

An Olympic Gold Medalist in track and field stumbled, fell down, and scarred themselves many times when they first started walking as a baby. And clearly their Gold Medal is proof that they never gave up on the idea of walking. That first step led to the next step and so on. Walking led to running, and consistent practice and visualizing crossing the finish line first led them to being recognized during the Olympic games as the fastest human being on the planet. And upon crossing the finish line the joy and thrill of the win surpassed all of the pain and effort experienced prior to that.

And although practicing may appear painful to onlookers, it's not to the one who enjoys the process. This Olympic star knows that the practice and work is simply part of the process that leads to massive success. The reward for your commitment supersedes anything that you can imagine. The harvest is always vastly greater than the seeds sown for the harvest. This is a scientific fact and cannot be modified. If you put in the work to create and live in the marriage of your dreams, you will meet at the appointed time exactly what you envisioned.

You and your spouse will stumble along this marital path. Keep in mind that you promised to live "happily, ever after". Ever after, is continuous and never ending.

Never put off for your marriage what can be done today. Not because tomorrow isn't promised to you, as what is often said. People use the phrase "tomorrow isn't promised to you" as an attempt to use the fear of death as motivation. But the truth is that death never inspires people to take action because people aren't afraid of dying until they are about to die.

Living in an unhappy marriage is agonizing. Therefore, procrastinating with your plans of a successful marriage causes anxiety about tomorrow because you feel that the next day will be exactly like today. And truth be told that's some scary shit.

And be aware that other people will copy what they see in your relationship. What if the fucked up marriage you're experiencing is the same tomorrow? Feel that! Thirty-days, 6 months, or this time next year you awaken in the same fucked up marriage, and still living unhappily ever after. How terrifying is that?

And guess who will emulate your relationship? *Yes, your children*.

Let's be honest, statically proven your children WILL NOT do *better than you*. Most children emulate their parents and will eventually mirror the same life experiences as their mom and dad or other couples in their immediate environment. If you're poor or rich, so will your children be poor or rich. If you're depressed, sad, anxious, and always unhappy, most likely your offspring will mimic the same behavior and emotional patterns. Your children are like a sponge, they absorb everything that they witness you doing, and once the pressures of life begin to *squeeze them*, what will drain out of them is exactly what they have soaked up while watching you.

All mistakes are but the mistakes of ignorance. Knowledge gaining and consistent use of this wisdom will produce a certain outcome. A lasting good, healthy, loving, fun, sexy and romantic marriage is possible once you accept that a good marriage is a reality, and obtaining the knowledge of how to create an exceptional marriage is what's necessary to enjoy living happily, ever after.

Ant's Five Compelling Reasons

Some people marry to lock down their spouse. One of my primary reasons for marrying Shira was to set her free. Free to evolve into her absolute best self, unhindered by any negative forces, for I am her protector. My goal has always been to help her grow and mature into the woman of HER dreams (not mine), and assist her with unfolding the gifts and talents that the Universe wants to express through her.

We've learned that there are spiritual benefits of a good marriage. Also, I was inspired to marry Shira realizing that living in a good marriage with her would allow me to see the world, as it really is: opulent, massively abundant, grandiose. A bad marriage distorts your view of life. It is limiting and traps you into small confinements emotionally and spiritually. And how you feel emotionally affects what you will experience in your reality. A bad marriage is blinding, because it keeps you from seeing and enjoying all that is available to you. But a good marriage is like being rich. Ahhhhh yes, being richly married...now that's another fascinating reason why we chose to get married.

To be wealthy includes living and experiencing an exceptional marriage; a sound, healthy, happy, loving relationship with your significant other. What does it prosper a man to gain the whole world and lose your soul...*mate*; to lose access to being spiritually connected with the love of your life. *Wealth,* is creating an abundant life that includes natural, mental, emotional, and spiritual opulence. You deserve to be happy.

You deserve to live happily, ever after. It is your birthright. Which is one more reason why we stood at the alter and before God exchanging vows to love honor and cherish each other until our last breath. You were born into this world to live the best life possible, and that includes a phenomenal marriage and loving relationship.

But our primary reason for marriage is because we like each other and are greatly in love. It's fun being married. I could not have uttered these words during previous relationships. It's so important to continue laughing with one another, carry on playing with each other, and never stop dating and treating your spouse as the person whom you hope to someday marry. Other couples perhaps, but for you and your spouse, living in your marriage is **not hard work**.

And with this mindset and commitment, the two of you at each stage in your time together will arrive year after year, tenderly holding hands while overcoming trials and tribulations, and creating loving memories that will last forever, having thoroughly enjoyed the **Married LIFE** ...until death due you part.

"*There is nothing that is either bad or good, rather how it's perceived that makes the experience for you bad or good*"

Elevate Your Marriage with Ant and Shira's 21 Daily Affirmations!

1. *I AM* so happy and grateful that I have learned to love myself; therefore, I am able to give my spouse the love he/she deserve.

2. *I AM* so happy and grateful for the power of life and prosperity expressed through each word that I speak.

3. *I AM* so happy and grateful to declare only that which I desire to experience in my marriage.

4. *I AM* enjoying a marriage that continues to grow stronger and more loving every day.

5. *I AM* so happy and grateful that my marriage is built on love, trust, and loyalty.

6. *I AM* so happy and grateful that {insert name} and I love each other with all of our heart, mind, body, and soul.

7. *I AM* so happy and grateful to be married to someone who is supportive and encourages me to fulfill my dreams.

8. *I AM* so happy and grateful that {Insert name} and I are more romantically in love than we were the day before.

9. *I AM* so happy and grateful that we love one another unconditionally and that our love helps us evolve into better people.

10. *I AM* so happy and grateful that {Insert name} is a true blessing in my life and an example of God's perfect timing.

11. *I AM* so happy and grateful that my marriage is a gift from God and an inspiration to many other couples.

12. *I AM* so happy and grateful that {insert name} and I are loyal, devoted, and committed to creating and enjoying the best marriage possible.

13. *I AM* so happy and grateful that my spouse adores me and feels admired by me.

14. *I AM* so happy and grateful that we share the same goals for our marriage and accept only great things for our relationship.

15. *I AM* so happy and grateful that our love and intimacy is renewed daily and that we fall in love with each other over and over as if for the first time.

16. *I AM* so happy and grateful that my marriage is fun and sexy.

17. *I AM* so happy and grateful that I attracted the perfect mate who enjoys my presence and that our friendship is revived daily.

18. *I AM* so happy and grateful that {Insert name} is faithful to me and I am 100% devoted to {Insert name}.

19. *I AM* so happy and grateful that my marriage is full of abundance, love, and compassion.

20. *I AM* so happy and grateful that we cherish, honor and respect each other.

21. *I AM* excited, happy and grateful to grow old with {Insert name} by my side living happily ever after.

"Marriage is fun and sexy." Follow us on Instagram:
AntandShira

"My Dream Is You"

I can hear the blossoms sing

And the hymns of the bumble bees

I can hear the whistles of the trees

The arioso rustle of its leaves.

I can see the rays of the sun

As it tangos with the wind

I can taste the harmony of the river

As our love sings songs that overflow its banks

Having you to love is my heart's constant thanks

I inhale your beauty, Dear Poem (Arabic meaning for Shira)

And I embrace your love

I wrap my eyes around your beauty, Dear Song (Hebrew
meaning for Shira)

As you embrace my love.

As I rest in the fields of our love's intimacy

I close my eyes in the peace of our love's divinity

As I watch the rainbow seal the promise of our love across the sky

I use its pot of gold to catch the tears of joy that flow from my eye!

As I find comfort in the deepest realm of my sleep

I realize that my constant thoughts through and through,

My imaginations, my visions, and my every *Dream is You!*

YouTube: **"LIFE with Ant and Shira"**
For relationship tips and advice, hilarious commentary
videos, world-class travel recommendations, visit our
channel to watch and share our videos; and subscribe
and hit the notification bell so you don't miss out.

www.antlamarsmith.com

www.ingramcontent.com/pod-product-compliance
Lightning Source LLC
Chambersburg PA
CBHW041412010726
47507CB00005B/244